AT THE RAINBOW'S VERY END
Stories for a Daughter

AT THE RAINBOW'S VERY END

Stories for a Daughter

By Franklyn Jones

This is a work of fiction. All of the characters, organizations, and events portrayed in this novel are either products of the author's imagination or are used fictitiously.

At the Rainbow's Very End

Copyright © 2014 by Franklyn Jones. All rights reserved.

Edited by Alissa McGowan
        Joanne C. Hillhouse
Cover Design by Kahari Cephas
Interior Design by Richard A. Dueñez

Printed in the United States of America

Published by GG LLC Publishing

http://www.AttheRainbowsVeryEnd.com

ISBN: 978-0-692-32413-4

No part of this publication may be reproduced, distributed, or transmitted in any form or by any means – including photocopying, recording, or other electronic or mechanical methods – without the prior written permission of the publisher, except in the case of brief quotations in critical reviews and certain other noncommercial uses permitted by copyright law. For permission requests, contact: fjones4044@yahoo.com.

Narcal! Me wan' see you, Rhonie! Apologize to Collie.

Thank you for all your help and your input.

Contents

Gutly's Revenge	3
The Island	8
The Walk	17
The Corner	26
Oxy's Weakness	35
Beady's Shopping Trip	42
Willie's Cutting	47
The Court Date	56
The Picnic	62
The Revival	77
Contact	84
The Corner Again	91
The Union Meeting	102
The Union Job	108
The Talent Show	116
Oxy's New Job	120
Oxy and Tricia at Work	130

The Match	134
Post Match	141
Tricia Chooses Oxy	145
Oxy Is Discharged	152
Oxy's Transformation	157
The Conflict	164
RayRay Reconsiders	169
The Union	178
Joy and Heartbreak	183
The Riot	191
Encumbered	198
Confrontation	203
Epilogue	209

Sweetheart,

    Here is a father's tradition, a window into the actions and behavior of the people in my childhood community. It was the 1960s, a time of precocious Caribbean leaders whose strengths and weaknesses were never in balance. They were determined, decisive, and independent, but their domineering personalities, derision of political compromise, dismissal of opposing perspectives, and failure at collaboration resulted in squandered potential and truncated development.

    Through this work of fiction, I will attempt to provide a glimpse of the people of that community and their social interactions, a look at the landscape of my formative years.

    My life revolved around school, Bayside, pasture, and bush. Bush was the place for weekend adventures. We spent our time there hunting birds; visiting the salt pond; and gathering mango, guava, sugar apple, cashew nuts and cashew fruit, stinking toe, cherries, sapodilla, and sugarcane.

    Bayside was off limits as a rule, because of our guardians' fear for our safety. But a day at the beach frolicking in clear blue water and cavorting on the white sand, catching blue crabs, pulling mussels, picking whelks, and using a puller to hunt snipes was worth the chastening that followed.

    The adults – family, friends, and neighbors – helped each other and shared food, mêlée, and responsibilities. On weekdays they made work or found it – baking bread and pastries, taking in washing, picking cotton, cutting cane; as fishermen, tailors, shoemakers, carpenters, masons, shopkeepers – and raised their children. On weekends, they drank a little, quarreled some, cooked big meals, and attended church.

    Our guardians worked hard to ensure our happiness and a smooth journey through life. Theirs were not lives of leisure and plenty but ones of hard work and improvisation. They were adamant that we use the public education offered by the elders of the island as our transport to a life that was better than theirs.

Many define poverty as a deficiency or a hardship, but if the defined poor do not recognize either in themselves, then poverty does not exist. There were numerous deficiencies and hardships in our lives, but we assigned poverty to someone in a foreign land. We were happy.

I give you these stories in the hopes that they will provide you with a little insight into the experiences and the community that influenced me during my foundational years. Enjoy.

Love,
Your Father

CHAPTER ONE
Gutly's Revenge

"Ah wha' ah go' on in deh?"
"Gutly, Rosie, and she keep-man ah argue."
"Yeah? This go' sweet."

A crowd was gathered outside Gutly's house, anticipating trouble. Inside, Gutly was engaged in a hot argument with his woman. Rosie was semi-retired after a long career as a weekend nighttime worker (and was of an age at which she should have been fully retired), but she loved the work and was always eager to earn extra cash. So she continued to substitute on occasions when FatSlim's Place needed help, and the night before she had gone out and returned home with Soby.

Gutly was aware of this, but he did not complain or make any comment about the strange man in his home. Instead, he left the house and stayed away for what he considered a reasonable amount of time, hoping that on his return, his woman would have come to her senses and her sweetman would have departed. Saturday night turned to Sunday morning, which stretched to past midday, but that apparently was not a reasonable amount of time for Rosie.

So on a peaceful Sunday afternoon, with his options few, Gutly chose vexation.

"Me not going to take this shit anymore. What you think, me stupid?"

His forceful words set the stage for pandemonium. The people present that day maintain that Gutly set it off by thumping Soby on the back of his head as he looked away. But folklore or not, blows were exchanged by the three involved in the fracas.

Gutly's bright white house was small but outstanding amid the even smaller houses in his neighborhood, which was in the community of Celadon on the island (in the British West Indies). The wooden structure was built with rough-sawn lumber and galvanized steel sheets. It had two sections: in the front, a bedroom and living room; and in the back, a dining room and second bedroom. The kitchen was in the backyard: a perfectly square wooden structure, unpainted, with a door, two windows, and a roof of corrugated galvanized steel sheets like the roof of the house.

The walls of Gutly's house were thin, the shuttered windows were always open, and the sounds of the confrontation blared out through the blinds. The other houses in the neighborhood were close, and very quickly Gutly's nosy neighbors swarmed over his front yard, and his backyard too. They then proceeded to jump in at every opportunity – all it took to get them going was a hint of acrimony and the sound of raised voices.

The ruckus inside the house excited the crowd in the yard, and with some cynical prodding from his more meddlesome neighbors, Gutly began prancing about with his chest out and his eyelids fluttering. Gutly was a blinker; he blinked at three times the rate of normal people and even more so when he was agitated.

As the size of the crowd grew, so too did the number of versions of what was taking place inside the house that afternoon.

"Me hear two sound, one briggadim biff and one bruggudum brap." Long Mouth Elaine reported in response to Palance's questions, trying to bring the sounds to life with her head, hands, and legs.

"Gut, bruk he neck! He forward; coming into yo' house and disrespecting you like that. I said break his neck!" Palance shouted, following the custom of switching from island dialect to English for impact, sometimes making the switch mid-sentence.

Let me tell you a little about Palance. His mother had christened him Stafford Brown, but he threatened bodily harm to anyone who attempted to use that name. Stafford was a fan of the American Western, especially the movie *Shane*. He was enamored of Jack Palance's character, the hired gun Jack Wilson, and borrowed the actor's last name. Palance was of average height, and had a dark complexion, scrawny legs, and a disappearing behind; his haircut was short in contrast to his thick bushy eyebrows, and the whites of his eyes were slightly yellow to match his jaundiced personality.

Palance was a talker – a real chatty fellow. He fancied himself a "bad John" and a cool cat. He was constantly causing trouble for his family and friends and was unique among troublemakers in having a list of nefarious misdeeds ranging from simple mischief to wounding with intent to commit larceny for pay. On this day, he was still dressed in his Saturday night clothes, the uniform of the low-roller gambler: a bright and colorful long-sleeved cotton shirt, gold chain, white Dacron-fiber pants, white belt and loafers, rings on all fingers, and a front-snapped-down, back-snapped-up felt fedora.

"Long Mouth, you know he? You know the man in ah Gutly's house?" Palance asked, his gaze focused on the house instead of on Long Mouth.

"No, me nah think so, but somebody say that ah one thiefing boy from Uptown." The manner of Long Mouth's answer, and her posture, was a signal of bad things to come.

The activity inside Gutly's house titillated the restless crowd, the sounds that poured from the windows heightening the atmosphere of hostility and impending mayhem – a blend that was pure entertainment to the assembled, who enjoyed every bit of it. Only live steel band music could have added to their delight.

"This is not going to end well for this Uptown boy," Palance said softly, before turning to walk through the crowd, asking questions over the sounds of the disorder. "Anybody know wha' de boy name is?"

He was facing away from the house, interrogating folks, when someone told him the trespasser's name. At that very second, he heard shouts and screams behind him and turned quickly to see Soby running out the back door, shirt in hand and shoeless.

"Get him!" Palance shouted, and moved quickly toward Soby.

The crowd, moving all at once, followed in hot pursuit, cussing, screaming, and shouting for retribution. Soby, a top-notch footballer, started well, and his fitness and practiced running gave him an unfair advantage, enabling him to maintain a comfortable distance between himself and the marauding mob. The crowd heaved, throwing all manner of missiles — bottles, stones, and tin cans, large and small — which were gathered from the bare dirt yards in their path.

Gutly's house was located on the top of Johnny Hill in the middle of Celadon, and Soby needed to run more than a mile to clear the boundaries of Celadon and reach the safety of Uptown. With leaps and long jumps, he quickly navigated fences, clotheslines, footpaths, short and narrow alleys, stone heaps, and brambles to get to the road that would take him down Johnny Hill. Palance, still leading the crowd, tried to keep up, and although Soby had to slow down to make a ninety-degree turn onto Baker Street as he went past Jane's Rum Shop, the mob had lost ground. Still, they would not relent.

Sunday was the day when the sanctified attended church and the hardworking went into semi-seclusion. All businesses shuttered their doors, and only those who provided essential services worked. People ate heavy breakfasts, special Sunday dinners, and listened to sacred music on the radio, but on the Sunday of Soby's frenzied flight down Johnny Hill, the angry and growing mob that chased him had no regard for the traditions of the Sabbath.

"Ah wha' he do?" a middle-aged woman – neither a sanctified nor a hard worker, heading in the opposite direction and balancing a basket of Sunday buns on her head – wanted to know.

"Why ya'll chase the man?" a playful youngster asked, before turning to join the animated crowd.

"He knuckle Gutly." The answer was prompt and came simultaneously from several angry voices in the crowd.

Little Len sat on his front steps and watched Palance's pitiful efforts to hit Soby with beer bottles, then decided with relish, and a smile, to join the fray. Little Len was celebrated for having the most precise throwing arm in Celadon. He excelled at all activities that required an even hand – playing marbles, playing cashew, and pelting bottles and stones – and he immediately raced to the front of the throng for a better look at Soby.

Soby maintained his pace on the even ground of a road without curves, which helped him to outpace his pursuers. He approached Swinger Pasture thinking that once he crossed to the Uptown end he would be safe. Little Len had a similar thought and sprinted ahead of the crowd with the perfect missile in his hand.

It was an oversized pebble from a nearby beach, smooth and almost round. You may doubt this version of the throw; that is your choice. But Little Len hurled his missile from a distance of fifty yards. His throw was off that day and his oversized pebble missed the target a bit, striking Soby on his upper back instead of his neck as intended. Soby fell to the ground about ten yards from safety but managed to raise himself, spitting dirt from his mouth, and gratefully amble away to rapturous shouts of gratification from his antagonists.

CHAPTER TWO
The Island

Gutly slept well on Sunday night, after Rosie left his house for the comfort of her sister's place. He woke up reborn and wanted to talk about it.

At Jane's, Oxy sat alone, thinking hard, sipping a sweet drink and having a quiet morning, when he saw Gutly approaching the entrance of the rum shop. He knew instantly that he was bound to hear a tale or two about FatSlim's duplicitous dealings, Gutly's broken heart, the ruckus at Gutly's house, and the transgressions of Rosie. It was the first day of the workweek, and Oxy was aware that over the preceding weekend, Rosie, who was the mother of Gutly's two children, had scratched a line through at least eight of the Ten Commandments.

It was late morning, and Jane had left Oxy to his solitude after serving his drink, disappearing into her residence at the back of the rum shop to complete her morning chores. The shop was not much – a musty little place constructed of lumber, typical of any rum shop in 1960s Celadon. It had an exposed ceiling, a roof made from corrugated galvanized steel sheets, and an uneven and unfinished concrete floor. On the left side of the structure, beyond a counter, a four-foot-wide, eight-foot-high doorway was cut into the wall that divided the rum shop from the residence. To the right of the doorway, the dividing wall was lined with shelves for displaying the liquor.

The counter, which ran across the room from wall to wall ten feet from the entrance, had a built-in door that you had to lift up and pull out to open. The front of the counter had a treated bamboo façade and the top was covered in pastel patterned linoleum. The remaining furnishings consisted of four bar stools and two wooden tables with four chairs each. Oxy occupied the stool on the far right. There was a state-of-the-art jukebox against the left wall, midway between the counter and the front entrance, and that was Jane's biggest attraction. There were two windows on the right wall, one on either side of the counter. The window behind the counter remained closed during the week but opened on Sundays with irreverence to the ban on Sunday liquor sales.

The people of Celadon purchased half the liquor they consumed from sellers who were comfortable committing a transgression or two and often sold cheap liquor smuggled from the nearby Dutch Antilles. Although Jane's place was not easy on the eyes even with her new jukebox, she possessed a liquor license granted by the authorities, which afforded her the privilege of selling spirits legally Monday through Saturday. That was the place where Gutly went to declare his intentions.

"Can you believe this woman, man? Me damn good to she, forgive she worthlessness, take care of she children, and she sister children too, even forgive she big sins, and she still trying to hurt me." Gutly sat on the stool closest to Oxy and his hands trembled as he talked. The aggrieved man worked as a taxi driver, transporting tourists mostly, and normally his speech would mimic what he believed was a Yankee accent, down to a slightly exaggerated nasal quality. But he was angry, and had reverted to his native dialect.

"I knew things were bad before you opened your mouth. I could see them blinking eyes while you were on the steps. Me hear 'bout the worthlessness yesterday," Oxy said with forced interest, then took a sip of his drink and scanned Gutly from head to toe. "Boy, you know, you too soft. Let me pour you one; Jane gone in the back."

Oxy rose and leaned over the counter to reach a bottle from which he poured Gutly a drink.

Gutly's real name was Elvin Thomas, but it was rarely spoken because of his splendid nickname, which was in reference to his distinctive gut – not a stomach, not a belly, but an ugly gut. He was short of stature, with a big head and a toad's eyes. On this morning, he wore a loose-fitting Morina (a solid blue t-shirt) with khaki shorts and buffalo sandals – open-toed with an open heel and made from water buffalo leather – with a toe ring. His friend Oxy, whose given name was George Stevens, was also dressed casually but a bit more stylishly. He wore Arnold Bennett continental pants, a paisley print long-sleeved shirt, and the ubiquitous buffalo sandals. If you lived in Celadon and could afford it – hell, if you couldn't afford it but wanted to be hip – you owned a pair of buffalo sandals.

"So wha' you think me should do?"

Oxy looked at his friend and saw consternation on his face. He grinned brightly. "Well, Gut, as them say, what gone bad ah morning can't come good ah afternoon; seem like with this thing, it gone way past afternoon. As a matter of fact, that whole day done and you already into another day."

"You know what, Oxy?" Gutly spoke with determination.

"What?" Oxy asked.

"Me go' do somethin' 'bout she, 'cause boy is boy and big man is big man – and me no be one boy, me ah one big man. Me need to take big man action." Gutly was up on his feet and pacing, nostrils flaring, body twitching.

"Gutly, calm down man," Oxy said, playfully raising his hands to signal *stop*. "Mind you, a man can be happy with any woman, as long as he does not love her. You ever hear that saying? I think is one of them colonial masters from the mother country said that. Calm yourself."

Oxy rocked his stool, amused by Gutly's behavior. Gutly calmed himself and sat back down. Both men quietly sipped their drinks for a while, listening to the number Oxy had punched on the jukebox, their thoughts going to where the music took them. Then with a smile, Oxy breached the tranquility.

"Boy, you taking the wrong approach to this. You love the woman, you weak for she; so take things in stride 'cause I know that you don't plan to leave she. Try a new approach; laugh at yourself. If you do that, then you don't have to worry about nobody else laughing at you 'cause you done have that job," Oxy recommended, and stood, eager to end the visit. "What you planning to do for the rest of the day?"

"I have two runs to make this afternoon, and then ah have to pick up someone at the airport tonight." Gutly had let go of the weight he had brought into Jane's, and was in an easy state. Both men stood facing each other before parting.

"Ok, man, me have to go up the road to check on my work schedule." Oxy bumped fists with Gutly, who left while Oxy hung back to shout back to Jane. "Jane, Jane, me gone. Put an extra drink on my tab; I will pay for the one that Gutly drink."

Jane was way in the back, where Oxy could not even hear her stirring about, but he knew that when her money was involved she was quite discerning; she would be aware that Gutly had had a drink.

Oxy walked out of the rum shop, and immediately began thinking about the circumstances of his own life. He was conscious; he had figured out his strengths, and recognized his shortcomings. He knew that he was an underachiever, and every time he thought about that, he could hear the admonitions of his aunty. However, he was not able to harness that knowledge and understanding for the betterment of his life.

"If I could just manage to have a run of good luck," he rationalized, "I'm sure that I could turn my life around. I know this. Aunty always say that I don't take the important things in my life seriously; that is why I have fathered children that I cannot support. I know that I can do the successful life thing; all I need is to catch a break. If I can go through several months without a misfortune in my life, I could be on my way."

Walking in the late morning sunshine, he summoned his voice of reason. He did that when he needed to fill in the gaps of his anxiety. There is always a high way and a low way available, but Oxy's ideals were those of a pleasure-seeker whose priority was self-gratification; and that was the low way. Oxy never felt the itch of ambition, although he was an accomplished vocalist; could play some cricket and, in fact, was celebrated for a most tantalizing square drive; and was a natural winger for the community football team. He had not completed formal education – that process had ended when he was sixteen years old – but he was smart. When he chose to use his brain, his reasoning was sound and his language clever. Oxy was an ardent reader of books, and had kept and continued to use the public library card that was issued to him when he was a schoolboy. Oxy's curse was his appeal: he had an almost effortless ability to initiate relationships with women – relationships that had a tendency to end in calamity.

Oxy lived with his aunt. She was a woman with a caring soul who willingly opened her heart and her home to relatives and friends in distress. She believed that trials and suffering strengthened a person, and offered support and sanctuary, even to adversaries in need of encouragement and inspiration. Aunty focused on the best in everyone. She believed that while one's past, the easy choices made, cannot be undone, the present provides opportunities to correct the things that were done badly, and to make the tough choices that were avoided.

Aunty was the sister of Oxy's mother, who had migrated to New York City, where Oxy had made and abandoned an attempt to join her. His mother's new life and lifestyle could not accommodate him, so rather than exist on the fringes of New York City, he returned to his beloved island. Because of his aunt's belief, she was moved to invite her nephew to share her home after his return.

Though his accommodations were sparse, they were clean and tidy and came at a minimal cost, so he had nothing to complain about. Oxy was happy living with his aunt, for whom he had a genuine affection. Aunty was an active church and union member, and both organizations provided opportunities to meet a diverse collection of new friends and acquaintances that, along with her goodwill, was good currency for her and her nephew.

Oxy worked as a stevedore. He loaded and unloaded barges at the island's commercial harbor. When the barges were in use, they were loaded with goods and pulled by tugboats to and from cargo ships that were anchored at the entrance to the harbor. The tugboats were also used for transport when the stevedores' worksite was alongside the cargo ships. However, the primary use of the tugboats was to maneuver the loaded barges through the crowded harbor. The stevedores' work was hard, especially when it was time to ship bags of sugar. Cranes were not common on the island, and the bags of sugar were loaded from the landside docks onto the barges for transport to the ships via sugar-bag brigades: a line of men lifting the heavy bags and passing them along.

The stevedores' work schedule was dependent on an imperfect timetable, since ships often missed their scheduled dates, and double shifts with little rest were often required. Oxy was the youngest worker in his crew, and seeing what the work had done to the older men around him, he was hopeful for alternative employment before the specter of a deepwater harbor made it a necessity. But he endured, because the people of Celadon were used to difficult jobs and few alternatives.

The people of Celadon lived lives of defiance despite their circumstances. Many of those lives were strewn with hardship and difficulties; there was not a single wealthy person, by any standards, within its boundaries, although one or two flirted with that fantasy. The majority had no illusions about who they were, and took pride in their many contributions to the island's culture. Some residents were bent, but in Celadon that was not held against them. Their children were smart, and, with the fabled skills of teachers Miss Richardson and Miss Matthew, the children of the community regularly won honors for claiming the highest number of the limited seats that were available at the island's selective secondary schools.

The community had its own set of rules. Where the rest of the island saw straight lines, they saw polygons, circles, rectangles, and triangles. They loved to skylark, and handled afflictions, setbacks and distress with easy imperturbability, in spite of the fact that in all matters economic and political they often received the sharp end of the stick. Yet every day they had fun and skillfully kept trouble on the run by bracing themselves with humor as they struggled to overcome the challenges of life.

The oval-shaped island was a place of innate beauty, its serene landscapes amplified by the delightful smells of tropical fruit and flowers. Gentle green hills rose in the south and southwest; even gentler and less green hills in the southeast, and except for the less-than-notable points of elevation dotted around the island, it was flat everywhere else. The island's numerous sheltered nooks, sandy-white shoals, sky-blue inlets, sea-green bays, deep-blue harbors, and beaches (which were back dropped by the charm of palm trees and tropical plants), when seen from an elevated view, were tonic for astute eyes. One island fable tells of a challenge that took a year's worth of days, at a rate of one beach per day, to discover the most beautiful beach on the island.

Water was stored in cisterns, tanks, barrels, and drums. Rainwater caught from rooftops supplemented the water piped in from the public reservoir when water levels were high, which was rare. During the mid-sixties, the island experienced a particularly brutal drought, which had a profound effect on everyday life. It was common for residents to walk for miles in search of running water, fill buckets, and carry them back home on their heads. Communal spigots or standpipes were located in every village and throughout the city in an attempt to make running water available to the public, but they remained dry for the most part. These freestanding pipes were embedded in a concrete base with three four-inch-high sides and an opening for the runoff. The standpipes were a great benefit when they provided water, but that was an erratic proposition. The availability of water could vary from three days a week to two days a week, and sometimes as little as one day per week.

During the drought it was the practice to place old buckets in line overnight, single file, starting at the back of the standpipe; this was done in an attempt to have an order to things when water became available. Folks would check on a daily basis, in the early morning or evening, and when the water was turned on, there was a system for sending word to neighbors. Most people honored the system, but there were always the bad eggs – ruffians and vagabonds who had no honor – and there would be cuts and blood when one of these fools decided to break the line and act stupid. The government of the day had its priorities, and providing citizens with reliable sources of water was not one of them. Instead, the completion of a deep water harbor was the number one priority.

The island's founders had built the capital around City Harbor, a scenic natural harbor and one of the five that adorned the island. City Harbor was not deep enough to accommodate the docking of large ships, and for many months its beauty was diminished by the constant presence of dredging vessels sucking sand and silt from the bottom of the harbor and dumping it into pristine coves and mangroves.

The business and political classes viewed the deep water harbor project with pride, and the rest of the citizenry, especially those who made their living in and around the harbor, had trouble envisioning the potential benefits. For the prideful it would modernize the harbor, for cruise ships would no longer need to use ferry boats from the mouth of the harbor to the jetty at the edge of the city. The citizens who made their living on and around the sea saw no value in these proffered advantages. Those folks saw the destruction of pristine beaches, the disappearance of certain species of fish and other edible sea creatures, the reshaping of the seaside landscapes because of dredging, and the near annihilation of the storied Rat Island.

CHAPTER THREE

The Walk

Oxy turned onto nearby Baker Street, on his way to review his posted work schedule at another rum shop located a half mile from Jane's. Baker Street was a much-traveled route in Celadon, and Oxy's simple plan to get to his destination as quickly as possible turned into a test of patience. There were neither sidewalks nor shoulders, but the walkers had no conflicts with the infrequent vehicles, although maybe an occasional bicycle rider would need to ring his bell. Folks walked everywhere and felt obliged to have chats with fellow wayfarers on their to-and-fro.

Baker Street was paved with concrete, as were most of the main roads in Celadon, and its houses were small and ages away from plumbing. In Celadon some – those without a bathroom being part of their house improvised. Public showers were used when water was available – men only – and also bathing structures built in the yard, close to the house with whatever vessel was practical as a tub. Most homes were not enhanced by any shrubbery, but there was the odd tree sometimes and, now and then, a stone heap and a bramble made from tamarind tree branches. Some houses were inhabited by enterprising residents who nurtured fragrant front-yard flower gardens. Some were painted with bright paint; others had rough, weather-beaten wood, worn and discolored from years of Caribbean sunshine and rain. Half the residents on Baker Street were renters at rates as low as two shillings – about twenty-four cents – per week. That was Oxy's world as he made his way to his destination.

On a good day, the walk along Baker Street was a slow trip with many human distractions. The nature of the people and the norms of the time meant that walkers beset each other with endless questions, numerous offers, and constant news flashes. A hearty greeting was never enough; the travelers expected to and did engage everyone who would listen, or had something to say.

Teddy the butcher was the first person Oxy met on Baker Street that day, and Teddy had a tale to tell about Sonny Boy and a pig. Teddy was a devious guy. His legend included a tale of low cunning in which he was the sole survivor of a mini-massacre. As the story is told, Teddy and his gang of butchers arranged to purchase cattle from a cattle thief and on the day of the transaction, they devised a scheme to shortchange him. What they did not plan for was the certainty that men who perpetuate vile acts shall inevitably suffer the fate of the detestable, and, on that day, providence came in the form of a cattle thief with a gun. The butchers thought they had an advantage in numbers, but the cattle thief also had a plan, and did not stop shooting until he thought that he had killed them all. It was an ambush in plain sight. Teddy reportedly survived because at the sound of the first shot he fell to the ground and played dead.

Teddy's legend also included the improbable claim that he was the only consumer of chicken – cheap, hard, inferior, barely legal liquor that was his preferred drink – who remained alive, healthy, and strong. All other frequent users had expired, or were close to expiring. The practically pure-alcohol libation defeated all who dared to drink it on a regular basis. It caused red mouths, fat faces, fat hands, fat feet, and exploded hearts.

Teddy got Oxy's attention with a loud "Hey Oxy," and in his hasty speaking style, related a story of how he'd gotten into trouble for selling pork made from a stolen pig. Teddy began with a stutter and his speech gave the impression of impatience. He was upset, but took a moment to compose himself before telling Oxy the story of Sonny Boy's pig.

Sonny Boy, a regular guest at Her Majesty's Prison, had performed an extraordinary trick during his last stay there. On the evening before his release, he stole a pig from the prison stock, and got it over the prison wall to await him. There are no known details as to how he managed to steal it, get it over the wall, and hide it out of sight and immobile until he was able to retrieve it upon his discharge, but that is not the point. He did, and on his release, Sonny Boy promptly offered to sell the stolen pig to Teddy, who, because of his love of the swindle, did not refuse. Consequently, Teddy was arrested and charged with receiving stolen property, which lead to a court date with a magistrate. Teddy was not a happy man and after telling Oxy his story, he decided to head to Jane's to settle himself.

"I have an appointment with a half-pint," Teddy said with disgust as he turned and walked away.

Oxy continued his trek along Baker Street with a wry smile after hearing Teddy's story. However, his smile soon disappeared and was replaced with concern for his employment. He needed money, and his last pay packet had been inadequate to meet his financial responsibilities: not only did he need to pay debts at Jane's, but he was also under pressure to catch up on his child support payments.

"Hey Oxy, how it going boy?" Van's boisterous voice pulled Oxy from his thoughts.

"Van," Oxy said, surprised to see him, and laughed. "Boy you nah supposed to be in de hospital?"

"Yah, was up deh, but you know there was this fête ah wanted to go to, and you know me, ah love me action. Me go head back to the hospital now," Van said with familiar nonchalance.

"So wait, man, you telling me, that th' hospital released you so that you could get a taste of some fête?"

"Noooo," Van sang. "Ah jus' leave," he continued with an indifferent shrug.

"Tell me, brother man, what about all them hospital things, all the tubes and other shit that they hook you up to up there?" Oxy's stunned look earned him a cheeky expression from Van.

"Me just pull them out and leave." Van's impish reply made Oxy laugh out loud.

"Boy, you mad! See you later," Oxy shook his head and walked on. As he continued on his journey, his thoughts again turned to his troubles. What was he going to do about the child support that he owed to Eve? He had fallen behind badly, and she had taken him to court.

Oxy and Eve's relationship predated her going around the bend and becoming familiar with the court system. She had been a defendant regularly, answering for various infractions ranging from perjury to more serious transgressions including larceny. She once took a neighbor's dress from her clothesline because, Eve later said, she had a dance to attend and the dress was perfect for the occasion. Eve had a larcenous heart but she was a beautiful woman, and that was all that Oxy had cared about when he met her. Oxy was obliged to pay a paltry sum for child support – a weekly amount of five shillings and two bottles of milk – but he had missed a few weeks of payments because of the inconsistency of his wages.

His aunt had counseled him that his love of beautiful women often replaced his common sense. She often reminded him that a life is the product of social interactions over time: from the parents we were born to, to the friends we select, to the mates we choose. Oxy was a smart and talented person who sometimes drifted into the company of dubious people who were headed in the wrong direction on a slothful journey through life. He understood the challenges he faced, but his erratic approach to life and these calamitous associations complicated those challenges. The things that tested his peers, he found easy; and the consequence was a man who did not dedicate himself, functioned far below his capabilities, initiated low-grade relationships, and often stumbled into bad situations.

"That girl not right, le' she 'lone," his aunt had said, when she had first heard of his interest in Eve.

The cheerful sounds of children having fun pulled Oxy from his musings about Eve and the court and his worries about work. "Miss Hughes, Miss Hughes, never refused take old leather and make new shoes."

"Tee-ling tee-ling the school bell ring, Miss Martin tie up she panty with string, the string go brap, the panty drop, tee-ling tee-ling the school bell ring."

The sounds were a verbal duel between the students of Miss Hughes's School – where boys wore yellow cotton shirts and blue short pants and girls wore yellow cotton blouses and pleated blue skirts; and the students of Miss Martin's School – where the girls wore checkered pink and blue cotton blouses and gray pleated skirts and the boys wore pink and blue cotton shirts with gray short pants. The children sparred at every opportunity, using rhymes that would have made the Rhymer (a community icon who composed rhymes at the command "Rhymer, gi' me one") proud. Oxy shook his head, smiled, and walked on. With school out for lunch, Oxy realized it was getting late. He needed to hurry, so he walked faster and tried to carry himself as someone hustling, but he was soon hindered by another voice wanting to be heard.

"Oxy, me wan' see you." Obadiah was emerging from an alley with one of his two brothers; there were lots of alleys in Celadon. Observing that Oxy was ignoring them, their walk turned to a canter in an attempt to catch up to Oxy and talk to him.

"Obadiah; me no ha' none time now; me in a hurry." Oxy had recognized the voice, and spoke to the man behind him without turning to face him. Obadiah was not a man of means but he always had enough to get his hair done, and to purchase hair ties to keep his conk (chemically straightened hair), in place. An aspiring entertainer with the flair of American singer James Brown, he insisted that people refer to him as JB, but most folks were not very accommodating.

"Oxy, me wan' see you," Obadiah repeated.

"An' me say: me no ha' none time now; me in a hurry," Oxy repeated.

"Me just wan' ask you if you really go' sing in the talent show?" Obadiah asked. He walked beside Oxy for a while, his brother at his side, before Oxy relented.

"Boy, me have to. Me broke, and me desperate for money anywhere, and anyhow me can get it." Oxy's voice was tinged with sadness.

"You go murder them with some Cooke, and some Wicked Pickett, right?" Obadiah asked, referring to American soul men Sam Cooke and Wilson Pickett. "Me hear that th' idiot from country that think he name James Brown go' be on the show," he added, his voice heavy with disdain.

"Ah ha, me go' do that, and you ah the only JB. Later." Oxy did not slow down, and Obadiah and his brother, Malachi, struggled to keep up.

"Goddamn, Malachi, before you slow me down, the answer is no to you first question, the answer is no to you second question, and the answer is no to your third question, since I know you getting ready to ask three questions," Oxy chided Malachi, who was obviously about to speak. Malachi was the youngest of the three sons of Zephaniah, known as Zeph, who had a penchant for naming his sons after minor Old Testament prophets – a practice that was popular at the time. Their other brother was Hosea.

"Me just wan' find out, if you plan to practice with the football team this year, and if you know that the Uptown people throw we out of the first division, and what you think go happen in the second division?"

"Three questions," Oxy murmured under his breath.

"Oxy, you should talk to your partner Beady about it, since he big in the team," Malachi suggested, his final statement in the one-sided conversation. Although Oxy was interested in Malachi's questions, he didn't want to waste time chatting.

The football authorities had come to a decision, in secret and with no legal reason, to relegate the Celadon team to the second tier of the football league, and thus the people regarded them as villains. The perceived disrespect was discussed in vexed tones throughout the entire Celadon population, football enthusiast or not, and everyone had an opinion on the nature of the affliction that should befall the football authorities.

The island was divided into three distinct sections: Celadon, Uptown, and Country (that's how the residents Celadon saw it). Football administration was the purview of Uptown, and the people of Celadon believed that Uptown folks viewed themselves as a higher form of human, dismissive of those who lived lives that were contrary to their precepts. They also believed that Uptown often made decisions and took actions that were prejudiced and high-handed. Uptown had annoyed them by not offering an explanation for the team's demotion, which reinforced the community's belief that the authorities were not only fearful of them but would also put every obstacle in their path to equality.

Oxy made progress, and was nearing his destination when he stopped to talk with his aunt, who was heading in the opposite direction. Although they lived together, and he had spoken to her before he left home, a quick greeting alone would not do.

"George, where you off to?" Aunty asked.

"Aunty, ah going up by LickFoot Stanley. I have to check the schedule to see when I go to work."

LickFoot Stanley's place was a step up from Jane's. It was a concrete structure with much better definition than Jane's and it was on a main thoroughfare where there was plenty of foot traffic. The patrons of LickFoot Stanley's place referred to it as a bar, not a rum shop, and it had tables and chairs for drinking patrons, domino players, and those who wanted to play cards or wari. There were enough stools for sitting, whether facing the counter or facing the jukebox. There was also a pool table and a foosball table. The floor was covered with tan ceramic tiles, and the structure was freshly painted.

The inside was green (walls) and yellow (ceiling), the outside sky blue with green trim. It was the Caribbean: a very colorful people, a very colorful place. LickFoot Stanley also provided his patrons with a wide variety of spirits; he sold many brands of imported liquor in addition to the domestic dark brown or white rum and the chicken that Jane's peddled. The bar was the product of LickFoot Stanley's retirement plan. He'd started out as a fisherman, and had managed to put aside enough of what he'd earned selling his fish (and smuggled liquor from his house) to open up the bar.

"Where you coming from? Jane place?" His aunt asked with a frown that made Oxy uncomfortable. "Me keep warning you 'bout all th' rum you drinking. Mind you, who won't hear will feel."

When his beloved aunt confronted him, Oxy was the picture of meekness, with the look of the admonished, and his fast talk and bluster was useless. Oxy's aunt was his signpost. She marked the way to the person that he hoped to become: as strong as she was, as kind as she was, and universally admired as she was.

"Aunty, is not like I'm a big drinker; I don't drink enough to get drunk," Oxy said meekly, and Aunty kindly changed subject.

"I keep forgetting to ask you, you hear anything about the case lately?"

"Nah, was just thinking about it, don't hear anything yet, Aunty."

"You pay that thiefing lawyer that you get?"

"Me still owe he some money."

"I don't trust that man at all, he love to take people money then don't show up in court for the case. Me just pray that he no do that to you." Aunty abruptly changed the subject again. "I don't know wha' happen to that girl Eve. In all my born years, me never see somebody stray so far from the straight and narrow. You know that girl use to spend she whole Sunday in church. She would start at Christian Mission at nine o'clock, then go down to Zion Church of God later that morning, then go to the Anglican Sunday School at three o'clock, then to Shiloh Gospel Hall or back to Christian Mission in the evening."

"Be not righteous overmuch," Oxy quoted scripture. "Maybe she and she parents should have paid more attention to wha' the scriptures say, rather than try to impress people with the number of times they went to church," he added dryly.

"I know that the girl didn't turn out too good, but going to church is a good thing. You should try and go once in a while. After all, I'm still paying the church society money for you." Oxy's aunt was neither a devout Christian lady nor a for-show Christian lady, but she was member in good standing in the Anglican Church and ensured that everyone in her family was in good standing with the Church also – at least on the books.

"Go on, go up to LickFoot Stanley. See you when you come home." Aunty paused and looked at him walking off, then went on her way.

Oxy breathed a sigh of relief when he looked down Baker Street and did not see anyone else ahead to interrupt him.

CHAPTER FOUR
The Corner

On his way to LickFoot Stanley's, Oxy had to walk past the Corner, which was located at the southwest entrance to Swinger Pasture – vocalized as "Swinger Pasur" by a people with a fondness for silent letters and apostrophized words – which was the place for sports: cricket (hard ball, soft ball, 'putian, and one tip out a man), football, and netball. It was also a place for meetings, church revivals, nocturnal erotic adventures, and other community activities.

Swinger Pasture was so named by the residents of Celadon because of its preponderance of swings. They also wanted to avoid using its official name, that of a dead British monarch. The conspiracy theorists enjoyed pointing out that when the perfectly square facility was built, there was a deliberate attempt to shut out the residents of Celadon. When the colonial masters and their proxies built the facility, the people of Celadon were not afforded easy access to it, even though it was located within the boundaries of their community.

Swinger Pasture was properly fenced, with two sides in Uptown and two in Celadon. The official entrances to the facility were two gates: a small, one-person-at-a-time gate, seldom opened, for foot traffic only, and the main entrance for large crowds and motor vehicles. Both were located on the Uptown sides of the fence. The conspiracy theorists said it was connivance. They saw easy access for the Uptown crowds, and difficulties for the Celadon hordes. However, the resourceful people of Celadon met that challenge by cutting unsanctioned entrances into the fence of the facility.

Swinger Pasture was one of the community's main meeting places; the Corner, near where the Celadon sides of the Swinger Pasture fence met, was another. When folks congregated on the Corner, they sat on or stood near the oversized steps of a weather-worn house of indistinguishable color across from a lamppost with the brightest light in Celadon. The step had a wide landing, built for accommodating plants but used for sitting and minding people's business.

While Swinger Pasture was the place for sports of all kinds, the Corner was a place where men gathered to hone their heckling skills and to be nosy. Women did not sit on the Corner.

Tortoise and Brap were the main tormentors and had the good seats. To earn a good seat, one had to be a chatterbox, well liked, a teller of jokes – at times ugly jokes – and a scandalmonger. Politics, economics, the direction of the community, the direction of the island – these were not topics discussed on the Corner, which was a place for insinuation and gossip. And the innocent and not-so-innocent pedestrians who passed by were easy prey. However, one of the finest traits of the folks of Celadon was not to take offense at words. People never felt put upon if someone said something untoward. Instead, they either ignored the affront or relished the opportunity to respond in kind. That's why the antics on the Corner thrived.

As Oxy approached, he slowed down and offered pleasant greetings to his friends sitting there. "Things ah-right?"

"Yeah, things ah-right," several voices responded. Though in a hurry, Oxy sat on the steps; the person he sat next to spoke.

"Look at that boy-for-Winston," said Tortoise, a tall fellow who wore size fourteen sandals and stood over six feet tall. He had been nicknamed Tallboy before it became near criminal to use that name. He had objected vehemently to the boy part of that nickname and ceased to respond to it. He had a distinctive round head with a square-top haircut, a cocoa complexion, and large eyes that were referred to as gobby eyes by his childhood friends. Tortoise's movements had a slow motion effect; he was a slow walker, which often made him the target of jibes.

"Hey, no do that, man; leave the boy," Brap snapped. Brap had very white teeth that were all visible when he smiled, a dark, smooth complexion that highlighted the whites of his eyes, a well-proportioned African nose, lips that would make Mansa Musa proud, wide shoulders from daily use of a carpenter's saw, and strong, thick sprinter's thighs supporting his five-foot-ten frame.

"But is true," Tortoise replied.

"You, Boy-for-Winston," Tortoise shouted at a youngster who was walking past on the other side of the street. Folks were inclined to walk on the opposite side of the street when they were in the area of the Corner.

"Me no belong to no Winston; me belong to Chris," the boy shouted back.

"Me say Winston ah you daddy, and when me say Boy-for-Winston, you suppose to answer me," Tortoise scolded, then added, "When you go home, ask you mother."

"Le' me 'lone," the boy said, and went about his business.

"Eh-eh, Tortoise, you hear the latest about Wacker?" Brap asked.

"No, tell me the tale," Tortoise said. Oxy had something to say on the matter of the boy, but held his tongue while Brap told his story.

"He live with a woman and still going out every night chasing other man woman," a smiling Brap said, feeling good about pivoting the conversation away from the youngster's discomfort.

"Tell me wha' happen, man," Tortoise said.

"Well," Brap said with a chuckle. "He was with some man woman up on Johnny Hill and the woman man stroke him with a bullbud."

"What!" Tortoise exclaimed. A bullbud is a mythical, magical tool used to lash a contrary man. It is used as a weapon or as a tool to punish. Folklore maintains that one stroke on the back of an adversary with the dried and stiffened bull's penis is enough to make that adversary do unpredictable things.

"So go on, tell me; tell me wha' happen," Tortoise said.

"Well, the man lash he with the bullbud, one lash, and he walked away calmly, whistling the melody for the hymn 'When the Roll Is Called up Yonder,' and went home to sleep," Brap said.

"Nothing 't-all go so," an amused Tortoise said.

"Well le' me relate exactly how it happen." Brap's smile was wide enough that all his teeth, top and bottom, were visible.

"Them say about three in the morning he wake up screaming, 'Murder! Murder! Throw water 'pon me!'" Brap paused, enjoying the moment before continuing the story. "'Wha' happen, honey?' his groggy woman asked, and he shouted again, 'Me say throw water 'pon me!' Then his woman said, 'Ah-right, ah-right, but the only water in the house is the good water (untreated rain water) in the jar-pot.' And he shouted, 'That even better; use that, use that,' and was still stripping off his pajama when the first cup of good water splashed in his face." Brap laughed the loudest at his own joke.

"It seem that th' lash he get was one of them delayed pain and hurt ones," Tortoise said, and even Oxy had a brief laugh.

"Tortoise!" Oxy said after Brap finished his tale. He spoke with a coolness that was felt by everyone present, turning the conversation back to Tortoise's earlier teasing of the boy. "Why you don't pick on someone your own size? Leave the boy when you see him. No bother the boy. Chris is me friend and his woman is me friend, too." Oxy looked at Tortoise as if expecting an answer before ending the reproach by saying, "Ah-right?"

Like Oxy, Tortoise, Brap, and the idlers on the Corner, everyone in Celadon had a proper name – the name recorded on their baptismal certificate and their birth paper. However, it was rare to hear the proper name of a young male spoken. Take Melo, the young man that approached the Corner as Oxy chided Tortoise. Melo, and all who earned that sobriquet (male or female), did so because of their distinctive mouths and resemblance to the most famous big mouth of the period, a calypso singer named Melody. His features were quite severe and his countenance and charcoal complexion elicited unpleasant words at first sight.

"You ugly, Boy-for-Pinky" Tortoise called out to the young man, who was heading toward Uptown.

"Me hear that you lose the job at the sugar factory. Wha' happen?" Melo knew that the question was mischievous, but he replied nonetheless.

"Them say that things slow, they keep me on as long as they could, but with the reduced tonnage that they producing there these days, and the worldwide competition, they no ha' no choice, so you see, me can't complain. When they had work ah had a shift," Melo said. The absence of malice or bitterness surprised Tortoise, and the tenor of his questions changed.

"Wha' you use to do up there?" Tortoise asked.

"Me use to work in the bagasse house." Melo said. He paused for a response, didn't get one, so he continued eagerly. "You know wha' bagasse be?"

"Me know you go' tell me, so go ahead," Tortoise said.

"Well, bagasse is the cane peeling fiber, left over when they done crush the juice from the cane, and the men in the bagasse house job is to sort it, and organize, and get it into the furnace to use as fuel." Melo liked to discuss his job, and was delighted that Tortoise showed interest in what he had to say.

"So you ah one bagasse boy," Tortoise joked.

"Yes I was a bagasse boy, and it was good work for good pay. It is a pity that th' sugar factory going down. I know that the new oil refinery will hire some people from the factory, put it's a pity because they hired th' majority of the professional and skilled people on the island and they pay th' best money," Melo said.

The fate of the sugar factory, once the power that drove the economy of the island, with major influence on culture and politics, was determined by the new realities of sugar production. The sugar factory could no longer match the production rates and prices of its competitors around the world and was falling behind fast. There was also the vision of the island's leaders, who could see most if not all of its citizens leaving the hard work and drudgery of the cane fields and other agricultural endeavors for better jobs in the island's budding tourism industry, white shirts, ties, and dress pants replacing flour bag or khaki shirts and khaki pants.

"So wha' you go' do?" Tortoise asked, looking at Melo with his hands raised in the *what?* pose.

"Well, all good things must come to an end. Now me will just find something else. Me still have th' boat, so me can go dive some lobster, or do a little fishing, pull some whelks, some cockle." Melo talked like a man with prospects. He carried a leather shopping bag, which he shifted from shoulder to shoulder.

"People say that since them start the dredging for the deep water harbor, fishing drop off and you can't even pull seines no mo'," Brap reminded them, then added, "Melo, that's how it is, changing times."

"Well me no know 'bout that, but me have to do something. Fellas, ah gone."

"Fellas, me gone too," Oxy said, getting up.

"You gone ah-ready? You just reach," Tortoise protested.

"Oxy, weh you in so much hurry to go?" Brap asked.

"Me in a hurry because ah going over by LickFoot Stanley—"

"Oh," Brap interrupted. "You go check you schedule. Ah-right, then, see you later."

"Tortoise, you remember them days when we use to catch mullet by han'? Remember, the incoming tide use to bring them into the mangrove?" Brap asked.

"Yeah, Brap, and we use to block them with bush, so that the receding tide wouldn't carry them out, and then just toss them out of th' water with bare hands. Them were the days."

"Yeah, that deep water harbor really mess things up," Tortoise replied, before someone caught his attention. "Oh gyde, look Casey coming down the road, me have one question or two for he, 'bout he sister, Gretchen. Me hear she get lockup." Tortoise used his chin to point out an approaching young man. He was not close enough for Tortoise to see his face, but he could imagine Casey's usually stern look – lips set tight, and eyes focused on anything except the gang sitting on the steps.

"Wha' she lockup for?" Brap asked.

"Me no know, but wha' me hear, is that they ha' she three days now," Tortoise said.

"Three days, and she can't get bail? How much so the bail cost?" Brap asked.

"Me hear thirty dollars," Tortoise answered.

"Thirty dollars!" Brap exclaimed. "But that no' much."

Casey was approaching the jokesters from the area of Swinger Pasture and he was dressed in good clothes – not quite Sunday best, but much better than his usual everyday khaki pants and t-shirt. Folks in his neighborhood viewed Casey as a dim bulb; in fact, that was his nickname.

Casey was one of the many young men from Celadon who'd left in search of better economic opportunities in the U.S. Virgin Islands, at a time when the islands were experiencing a severe labor shortage in both their service and construction industries. The Virgin Islands' administration had actively sought help by dispatching representatives to recruit workers from neighboring islands. Young men like Casey left their homes and set out for St. Thomas and St. Croix by air or by sea. The active recruitment of workers lasted a year, but five years after the initial call-up, large numbers of uninvited job seekers were still traveling to the Virgin Islands. U.S. Immigration disapproved and implemented a program of roundups and mass deportations of the undocumented. Casey's story, as it was told, was this:

While living in hiding, Casey heard a rumor that immigration officers had suspended their efforts to hunt, apprehend, and deport illegal residents, so he decided to make some inquiries. One day, he left his hiding place, went to a supermarket, and met a uniformed immigration officer while walking in the parking area. Casey boldly approached the officer, got his attention, and began his inquiry.

"Mister Immigration," Casey said, polite and respectful.

"Yes?" the immigration officer replied.

"Is true you all stop sending home aliens?" Casey asked.

"Why do you ask?" The officer's manner was neutral.

"Because some people tell me so, and me no want to hide no more," Casey explained.

The officer detained Casey on the spot; he did a brief stint in a holding facility, got a court hearing, and was deported to his homeland.

"Dimbulb, me hear you sister lockup, ah true?" Brap asked when Casey got close enough. Casey didn't stop and did not answer. He never answered, since his inquisitors had, in the past, taken great pleasure in giving him grief. This day was no different, so he continued on his journey. Every time they saw him, Tortoise or Brap would ask Casey to recount the story of his encounter with the immigration officer. The veracity of Casey's story was questionable, but they loved it because it was commonly believed that Casey himself was the originator of the tale, and that he belittled himself by relating it.

Casey's jaw was set when he walked by the steps. He looked straight ahead, his gait urgent, but even with that attitude the guys on the Corner were not done.

"Dimbulb, you not answering me today?" Brap pressed. "Me hear Gretchen lockup fo' three days now, and she can't get bail money. Me hear that th' bail is thirty dollars, but she only ha' twenty eight, and she can't get th' two dollars to make up." Not waiting for Casey to respond he continued, "Wha' happen, she don't know anybody, or she so terrible that nobody want to give she th' two dollars so she can get out?"

By the end of the exchange – well, it really was not an exchange because Casey never said a word – he was beyond them and well on his way home.

CHAPTER FIVE

Oxy's Weakness

Oxy was on the road to the bar when his thoughts drifted back to things in his life: the women involved and those troublesome relationships. Some men in Celadon had two families and the means to provide a home for each, with the homes being in close proximity in many cases. Oxy did not have that luxury; he had the relationships but not the means.

Plantation owners had stamped out most of the traditions brought to the island by the Africans during centuries of British domination before emancipation. However, remnants of the language survived and were used in daily conversations. So, too, remained the vestiges of houses built in the African tradition. Also, for some men, the tradition of having multiple families, the practice of polygamy: a tradition that had passed with the times of their ancestors and had no place in 1960s life, yet still it survived. The women who were the martyrs of this inequity practiced self-restraint; although they lived in a place that celebrated rebellion – *selective* rebellion – women were not expected to rebel. They were the mortar that cemented the Celadon family, and were celebrated by their sons and daughters despite men who attempted to boost their manhood by embracing a backward practice.

No, Oxy did not have the means, but nevertheless he wooed various women and, tipping his hat to Abraham, was the father of four children: two by Rachel; one by Eve, who'd sued him for child support; and one by Rose, who had taken their child and left Oxy and the island for a life in Montreal.

As Oxy approached LickFoot Stanley's, he saw his best friend approaching.

"Beady. Beady, what's hanging over you?" he shouted and continued walking.

"Cockspur," his friend replied cheerfully.

"No, make Old Oak wait 'til Cockspur come," Oxy said, and both men laughed and hugged each other.

Cockspur and Old Oak were brand names of the most popular rums in Celadon at the time, and the reference was their unique way of acknowledging each other. You see, Oxy and Beady were part of each other's first memories. Their mothers were best friends before they were born, and the bond between the women was so strong that even their longtime friends thought they were sisters. Cathleen and Dianne had become friends in primary school, gone to typing class and secondary school together, developed an interest in boys together, and grown into womanhood together. As young women, they had borne and delivered their sons less than one year apart.

Oxy and Beady borrowed their greeting from a childhood game of recall and good guesswork. Here is how the game was played: A group of children gathers, and they choose a Questioner and a Beady. The game begins. The Beady lays, face down, eyes closed, across the lap of the Questioner, while everyone else searches their surroundings for an item that they can safely place on the Beady's back, then stand in line for an opportunity to do so. The first in line holds, for example, a sugarcane peel over the Beady's head, and the questioner asks, "Beady, Beady what's hanging over you?"

"Milk can," the Beady makes a guess.

"Let cane peel stay 'til milk can come," the Questioner says, as the sugarcane peel is placed onto the Beady's back. Then the next person in line holds his or her item over the Beady's head. The question, answer, and piling on sequence continues until the Beady guesses correctly and is released and replaced. A young Tyrone Frederick was the best at the game, guessing correctly more often than not, and in time he had the name Beady bestowed upon him, which he embraced because he disliked his given name.

"You come check the schedule?" Beady asked, as the friends approached the entrance of LickFoot Stanley's.

"Yes." The earlier jollity was gone from Oxy's voice.

"You schedule to work soon?" Beady asked, picking up on Oxy's change in demeanor.

"Yes, four days over the next week," Oxy said after he finished reading the schedule, which was posted on the inside of an open front-door shutter. "That good, but it could be better. Me really need some money right now. Me have child support to pay and lawyer fee to pay and things real tight these days." He punctuated this dispirited commentary with a loud groan.

Oxy did not mention the fact that he was worried about the disappearance of his job. He knew that with the completion of the deep water harbor, most stevedore jobs would vanish – as the job of the town crier, Bigfoot Abraham, had vanished; as the jobs of blacksmiths had vanished, like his cousin Dam-gutter Stan, who was broken when horse-and-carts, and thus his forge, ceased to be a part of daily life; as the jobs of his neighbor Rra and his fellow porters, whose carts until recently had transported goods throughout and to the outskirts of the city, were vanishing. Although he was a smart person, Oxy lacked any marketable skills – and in a marketplace dominated by tradesmen and skilled labor, his lack of a trade was a handicap.

"Yes, boy, things rough," Beady commiserated.

"No more cane to cut, no more cotton to pick. When workers realize that plenty people go' lose what little work that they could find…"

"… some ah them go' bawl," Oxy completed Beady's statement, shaking his head, genuine concern dragging on his face.

Beady enjoyed offering his thoughts on the prospects for workers in the community. "And you know, Oxy, soon them cotton fields to the west of the school will be wide open pastures; people will be using them for football field and cricket pitch." Beady realized that Oxy was moved by his impassioned words and went on. "And you know, Oxy, when them cut the cane field to the north of the school, they not going to cut no suckling (the stalk from the plant used for replanting) this year – won't need any; they don't plan to replant. Boy, things will be bad all around."

Both men walked away from entrance of the bar to stand in the middle of the street. That's when Beady saw a familiar look in Oxy's eyes – a look that had been the cause of bad things in the past. Oxy faced Beady, but he did not look at him; instead, his gaze was fixed beyond, on an attractive young woman walking toward them. She was dressed in a solid light-blue, drop-waist, knee-length dress with a crew neck and short sleeves, and she was beautiful, with slightly protruding lips, lively eyes, eyelashes to match, eyebrows to envy, a soft 'fro, a look that said, *I know I'm beautiful but don't bother me about it*, and the particular complexion that Oxy favored.

"Oxy, she too young for you, and she is a good Christian young woman; no bother she," Beady beseeched his friend. "With all the problems you have with woman, that young girl is trouble; don't be ridiculous."

But Oxy did not hear a single word. He was preparing his opening line.

"Hello, young lady," Oxy said as the young woman was about to walk by. He realized immediately that his greeting was weak – three worthless words – so he tried again. "Ah not too good with numbers, but ah know a figure eight when ah see one."

Oxy knew before he finished his line how juvenile it was, so to avoid slipping further, he did a shrewd thing and decided to be quiet and just stare. The young woman ignored him completely and continued on her journey. She was not about to engage in a conversation with a man she did not know, and who was standing in front of a rum shop. She also had no interest in a man who was not her age. Most importantly, she wanted to avoid the resulting uncomfortable reception she'd be bound to receive when she arrived at her aunt's house if she did. She knew that her aunt would be able to quote chapter and verse of every version of the encounter as related to her by nosy neighbors.

Gathering information – minding other people's business – was a special skill set in Celadon. Some folks gleaned all the news they could and stockpiled it – no wayward conversation ignored, every scuttlebutt treasured. News, rumors, and fabrications were passed on with glee. So some person, or two or three different persons, would have beaten the young woman to her home and informed her aunt of what they did not see and what they did not hear.

"Oxy, me implore you, leave that girl alone," Beady begged, but Oxy had lustrous eyes, and he was weak – a coconut bough in the path of a high wind. Hopeless.

"I don't know your name but I will find out soon enough, and we will talk again," Oxy called out to the young woman as she continued on her way. Beady gave up trying to talk sense into his friend and decided to continue on his errand.

"I'm going to the market, I need to buy some can cup; Willie cutting next Sunday and I promise to get some cups for he," he said, turning to leave.

"By the way, you know she?" Oxy asked.

"It don't matter whether me know she or not," Beady replied impatiently.

"Okay, Beady, I'm gonna split too. I will see you later." The two slapped palms.

"Go easy," Beady replied, and the men walked off in opposite directions. But then Beady stopped, turned, and said to Oxy's back, "Oxy, for you that girl is a poisoned chalice. I know her but I will not give you any information."

Oxy heard but did not turn, just raised and waved his hand and kept on moving toward home. It was only about a twelve-minute stroll to Oxy's place, but the sun was heating up, causing him to sweat. Oxy loved to look sharp and he had a reputation for being a cool cat. However, on that sunny afternoon, the tan continental pants that he had carefully picked out earlier in the day to go with the pink paisley long-sleeved shirt were proving uncomfortable with the sun at its hottest. Oxy had to walk to the top of Johnny Hill, and he was beginning to rue his choice of clothes. The sweat would certainly soil them by the time he climbed the hill, even if he maintained a leisurely pace.

"Aunty, me home; you here?" Oxy inquired, as he stumbled taking a shortcut over the stone-heap when he arrived home.

"I'm behind the kitchen hanging out some clothes."

Oxy had begun to walk toward her voice when his aunt came into view, wiping her hands on a white apron, then using it to mop her forehead. Aunty was dressed in a colorful skirt with a pattern of egrets and pink leaves on a yellow background. The skirt was Aunty's favorite. She wore it with a short-sleeved, blue, V-neck cotton blouse. Both the skirt and the blouse were from a Christmas box shipped to her by her son who lived on one of the U.S. Virgin Islands.

"One letter come for you."

She walked past him to a drum with a base of four concrete blocks positioned against the side of her house. Aunty unhooked a large can-cup dipper made from a cheese tin from a pot hook on the side of the house. She raised the lid from the drum and took a quarter-cup of drinking water, which she poured into her favorite enamel cup and drank with deep sighs.

Oxy went inside and picked up the letter from a small table that was one of four pieces of furniture in the room. The rest was comprised of a sturdy five-shelf bookcase, a two-back chair with the two backs joined at a ninety-degree angle, a table, and a bed consisting of a twin mattress on a metal cot with spotless, crisp sheets and pillowcases. Posters adorned the wall: Malcolm X, Martin Luther King, Jr., Angela Davis, and a sketch of Toussaint L'Ouverture.

"Shit." Oxy slammed his open palm into the center of the table. "Me no ready for this," Oxy groaned, as he looked at the notice of a court date on the table.

CHAPTER SIX

Beady's Shopping Trip

After Beady split from Oxy, his journey, though not long, was eventful. It took him past the Corner, through Swinger Pasture, and would have continued out the big gate. However, upon entering the pasture he was confronted by persons wanting an update on the status of the football team.

"Beady, wha' we go' do 'bout the disrespectful treatment that our team and our community getting from the football association?" Samson asked. Samson was the Celadon football team's unofficial historian. He sat with a group of four men, lazing under a tree in the afternoon shade.

"We working on it, but the fact is, they are the power and the authority and it looks like we will have to walk past the old cemetery to play our games next season." Persistent questions about the football team were wearying Beady, but he always responded with patience and told the facts.

"But that no right." A fortyish-looking fellow who was of Samson's generation joined the conversation, loudly.

"Beady, what about our representative; the Honorable?" Samson asked. "Every election he come down here asking us for help, for our vote – is time he do something for us."

"Sam, you have a good idea, I didn't even consider that," Beady replied, his energy back. He sincerely believed that Sam's suggested approach to the problem had some merit. "I will certainly work on that. But fellas, I need to get up to the market so we will talk later."

Beady walked off, toward the far end of the pasture and the big gate and the market. Samson and his friends would remain in the pasture for several hours. It was early afternoon, the island sun was warmest, and the shade of the whitewood tree and the comfortable breeze that was blowing across their bodies was perfect for their afternoon rest.

Beady's journey to Redman's was without further delays. Redman was a tradesman who practiced his craft outside the walls of the market. And every year, one week prior to Willie's cutting, Beady went to him to buy can cups. Redman produced the finest utensils, which included can cups, cake pans, and milk saucepans. Noted for his neatness and the quality of his products, Redman was first among tinsmiths on the island. He was one of the vanishing breed of tradesmen, something that Beady thought about and talked about at every opportunity. Redman's skills were of the highest order, but the demand for his cups, pans, pails, and flowerpots made from discarded tin-coated food containers, and for the repair of slop pails and chamber pots, was in decline.

As Beady neared his destination, he reminisced about a time when the people of Celadon were able to purchase most of what they needed within their own community, not having to leave their neighborhoods or their homes. He smiled as his mind filled with the sounds of criers, who were sometimes named for their cry, announcing their presence to the neighborhoods and broadcasting the wares they were peddling.

"All you, me a throw 'way mine," was the cry of Throwaway, touting the giveaway prices of her wares.

"Get you fish," was the cry of GetYouFish, who pronounced the word "get" as if it was one word with three syllables. GetYouFish became a renowned resident of the community after she prepared a special meal of rice and peas and stewed fish for her man's dinner. The storytellers say that when Saga sat down to have his favorite stewed angelfish, it was not delight but dismay that defined his meal. GetYouFish had a special fondness for drink and had indulged herself prior to preparing the meal, which affected her memory and caused her to serve her man his fish with the scales on.

"Get you coconut oil," was the cry of the physically challenged woman, who announced her product as slowly as her gait.

"Take you foot off ah that and put it on this," was the cry of the floor mat maker Buda, who was a big, tall man with a powerful voice to match his size.

"Get you chocolate nutmeg and spice," was the cry of Miss Rita, who had good vocals and could have been an opera singer.

Beady chuckled aloud when he remembered the short cries. The short ones were his favorites.

"Ladies," was the cry held for a full eight-count in the tenor of the meat seller on Sunday mornings.

"Cho-co-late," was the sweet cry of the diminutive Miss Ivy, who had a high-pitched voice.

Beady remembered fondly the sight and sounds of all the criers as they walked up and then down Johnny Hill and all the other neighborhoods, traversing every street, alley, and lane; or went door to door like any good peddler. But he had to quickly end his visit to the past when he arrived at his destination ready to do business.

"Redman, how much ah them shilling cup you have to sell me today?" Beady stood across from Redman, who sold his wares from behind a table that was barely adequate as his counter.

Now, do not imagine a fancy stall, because Redman's concession was not that. It was a square wooden frame, which he erected anew every day when he arrived to do business. The roof was tarp and hung over the sides when there was rain but was normally rolled up and tied off. Most of Redman's wares hung from the frame of the stall, and in the back was a workspace for his anvil, coal pot, hammers, and nails.

"Beady, me no have none shilling cup. You come buy from me once a year and you expect the same price as the first time you come here, five years ago," the tradesman replied with chuckles and smiles.

"Redman, I don't care wha' you say, those are a shilling apiece." Beady smiled too.

"Just tell me wha' you want t'day and how much," Redman said. "I forget wha' you tell me last week." He walked to where his wares were displayed and began unhooking the items that Beady would be purchasing.

"Give me five big cup, twenty-five of the medium-size ones, and twenty-five of the small cups." Beady gave his order – the same order he had given Redman when he was on his way to the gutter barbers for his biweekly haircut.

The gutter barbers trimmed hair at the outlet of Dam-gutter. Dam-gutter began at a small dam, which managed the run-off from the hills on the east side of the city. The barbers set up in the shade of the trees that were on the north side of a wide estuary, but the island's tendency toward drought meant that the barbers had to contend with nothing more than a gentle stream of water that flowed through the gutter and into the nearby sea. The barbers worked Saturday mornings and brought all they needed in small grips to their open-air shop.

"Come on man, is the order that me tell to you 'bout last week," Beady said. Redman had begun putting Beady's order together and ignored him until he was done.

"Wha' you fussing 'bout; you cups ready. Here!" Redman passed two large bundles of cups, tied together with Bristol twine, over the makeshift counter.

"I don't know how you going to manage all that, man," he added, then stepped back to watch Beady attempt to organize his load.

"See you," both men said in unison, but Beady's goodbye was muffled as he raised his unwieldy burden.

Beady managed to settle his cargo, then began his walk home, but he was not comfortable. He walked only a short distance before shouting at a young man directly ahead.

"Serendipity! Serendipity!" Beady shouted. "Serendipity, wait."

A teenager wearing casual clothes – work pants, t-shirt, and hoppers – stopped and turned around. Serendipity was so nicknamed by his maternal grandmother when he was born to her first child, the oldest of three daughters, who had delivered her miracle at an advanced age.

"You look like you need some help with you load," Serendipity said as he walked toward Beady.

"Boy, you nickname well suit you; me really need some help with this." Beady handed over half of his load to his friend, who suggested that they head back to Celadon.

"Me with you," Beady replied.

CHAPTER SEVEN
Willie's Cutting

Cheeriness in the early morning, especially on the weekend, was not Oxy's specialty; he was normally an exhausted man getting ready for bed. But it was special day: the day of Willie's cutting. Oxy had always enjoyed the period when farmers harvested their sugarcane crops, so he committed his Sunday to Willie.

Beady had been assigned the task of picking up bread for the lunchtime meal, but he had reassigned that task to Oxy. Oxy had agreed to do it because his place was closer to Maisy Gilliard's baker shop than Beady's, and although carrying the basket of bread would be a chore, Oxy felt good about it because he was helping his best friend.

So when Oxy woke up early, dressed appropriately, picked up a list provided by Beady, and left for Maisy Gilliard's baker shop, he was cheery. The list was simple: twenty two-pence loaves, twenty-five six-pence loaves, and fifteen shilling loaves. Oxy's job was to go to the baker shop, pick up a basket of bread, and deliver it to Beady's house. He knew that a full basket of bread was an awkward load, but he was committed.

Oxy had to enter the oven area to talk to Frank the baker, and although he had a fear of baker-shop ovens, he did not shrink from the visit. Oxy's issues with ovens were the result of a childhood accident. He had wandered from his mother's side while they were visiting one of her friends at a baker shop and was struck on the chin by the back end of the baker's peel. The blow was a result of the quick backward jerk of the peel, the technique used to dislodge loaves from the oven, and it had been forceful enough to split his chin and knock him on his back, half-conscious.

"Frank, morning." Oxy breathed heavily at the entrance of the eighteen-by-twenty-four-foot oven area before crossing the threshold. The main feature of the room was the brick oven – real red bricks, eight to ten feet high, with openings for the bread, the fire, and for removing the ash. The wood for the fire was stored on the floor along with bread baskets, ready for use.

"Hallo, man," Frank replied, not turning to look at Oxy as he withdrew loaves from the oven using a flat-tipped peel, and then guided the bread into a bread basket on the floor below the oven door.

"Frank, I didn't realize that them boys deliver wood on Sunday?" Oxy asked, referring to the men and the truck loaded with wood that was parked outside. "They say to tell you that them come," Oxy added, and Frank walked outside.

He hurried back in a few minutes later, complaining.

"Aahhhh, them fool stupid enough to come when me ready to pull bread from the oven. Ah start using some new fellas to deliver wood. If it was me old woodman he wouldn't show up today because he would still be drunk from last night. Me go set you up soon, gi' me fifteen minutes."

Frank groused a bit more about his new woodmen, then resumed his work, quickly pulling and dropping loaves into baskets with masterly control of the peel. Oxy watched him, and speculated on how much time and practice was required to master the skills that Frank showcased, deciding which loaves were baked, pulling them without nicking them or the loaves still in the oven, and dropping them expertly in the baskets.

"Oxy, Beady didn't order any bun, but me go' throw in some for he."

Frank put Oxy's order together by pulling the loaves from their baskets, which were assigned by price, and placing them into Oxy's basket.

"That good; I will eat one of them buns as soon as I get to Beady house." Oxy licked his lips and rubbed his hands together. "Nothing taste better than hot bun and cheese. Beady love bun and cheese, so he must have cheese in he house."

"Oxy, me ready; you ready?" Frank asked, gesturing for Oxy to come over to where he had efficiently packed the basket in less than the promised fifteen minutes. "Le' me help you up with this – you sure that you can manage?"

"Yah, man, just gimme a hand to put this basket on me head," Oxy said, and he grabbed a handle while Frank held the other one, and together they hoisted it onto his head. Oxy thanked Frank, and although his load was just on the wrong side of comfortable, it was an easy ten-minute walk to Beady's from the baker shop. Oxy arrived at Beady's place a little short of breath, but feeling good.

"Sister Ruth, me see you up." Beady had let Oxy into the house, and he was two steps inside when he spoke to Beady's woman, who called back a greeting from the kitchen. Then he requested, "Beady, help me down with this."

Beady and his woman lived in a neat, two-bedroom yellow wooden house with a kitchen and small dining room. It was located catty-corner from LickFoot Stanley's bar, with a small backyard and a well-kept front yard.

"You go' help me pack the bread by price into them marked paper bags that ah have hanging near the window?" Beady asked as they maneuvered the basket to a table in the narrow dining area.

"Me will get to that as soon as me put teeth to one of them buns," Oxy promised, rubbing his hands together in anticipation.

Dawn was just breaking by the time Oxy and Beady walked into the controlled din at Willie's "grung" (the name used to identify the plot of land that Willie leased for a fee and a percentage of the take from his crop), but there was enough light for the various crews to begin their preparations for the day's activities. The women were setting up the hearthstones for the cooking fires and unloading their pots, pans, and foodstuffs. The men were either getting dressed in the proper clothes for cutting, organizing, or doing some last-minute sharpening of their machetes, bills, and cane-knives on the whetstones that were set up near the cane field. The bread and other items that Oxy and Beady carried were handed over to the cooks and both men went to ready themselves.

Willie's grung was just under five hundred acres, and was green with sugarcane and a few large trees that provided fruit and shade. Ten minutes passed before all the cutters arrived and the rising sun's first rays appeared in the eastern sky. The cane cutters organized and positioned themselves to achieve the most efficient use of resources and time and began swinging their machetes and bills fifteen minutes after Beady and Oxy's arrival.

As they moved forward, the cane field began to change color from green to tan; the lines of cutters moved with intent, slashing off the cane top, cutting at a consistent length from the root, clearing it of leaves that remained, cutting the suckling, dropping it, and moving along. Their graceful movements were performed to a one-two-three-four cadence. The lines of cutters, the quickness of their movements, and the falling sugarcane when viewed from a distance rendered the effect of a wilting target under an irresistible force. The harmony of sounds and motions continued at a lively pace, with pauses for water breaks facilitated by the young ones carrying vessels for holding and drinking to the line of cutters. This continued until the sound of the lunch bell signaled the one formal break of the day.

The lunch break lasted an hour, and during that hour some of the men took naps while the women and children piled the cut sugarcane into large heaps, with a special heap for the suckling, which would be planted in furrows at a future date. The lunchtime feast consisted of kiddie stew, made with young goat's meat, beef in a thick brown stew, white rice, cabbage and carrots, and the bread Oxy had picked up that morning. The hot drinks were balsam and fever-grass tea; the cool drinks were water, ginger beer, and mauby.

Remember Palance? He was a top-notch cutter. His skill with the bill and the cutlass gave him high marks in the cane-cutting brotherhood, but his nasty disposition was notable as well. Because of his aggressive nature, he had been one of the first to walk through the nearby lunch line, and was now balancing his lunch vessels unsteadily while looking for a suitable place to sit.

"Oxy, we are looking good, we making good progress."

Oxy, who was on his way to the lunch area with his partner Beady, stopped and turned to the voice. He looked into the noticeable yellow tint of Palance's eyes and stopped to listen to what he had to say.

Beady walked away, to the lunch line, where he started to banter with Miss May.

"Miss May, the beef stew look good today. How it taste? Wha' the verdict so far?"

"Boy, no bother me with you ignorance, you know me no cook stupidness."

"If you say so, Miss May, if you say so," Beady conceded, smiling. Miss May was the cook but she did not serve, so Beady took an enamel bowl of beef stew, rice, carrots, and cabbage with his left hand, and a medium-sized enamel cup of balsam tea with his right hand from Aunty, who was a server. Aunty had been Willie's woman when they were young, and they had remained friends throughout their lives.

"Where is that nephew of mine?" Aunty asked.

"He's over there." Beady used his chin to point to Oxy and Palance, who were standing near a mango tree.

"Me hear that you trying to mak' a move on me cousin," Palance said, shifting his eyes and using a tone that was far different from that of his earlier greeting.

"Who is you cousin?" Oxy asked, matching Palance's attitude.

"Me aunty niece, Tricia," Palance declared loudly.

"Tricia? Who that?" Oxy did not raise his voice but gazed steadily at Palance.

"Yes, Tricia. The young lady you try fuh trouble outside of LickFoot Stanley the other day," Palance explained, his swagger on full display.

"Oh she, who tell you that me try fuh trouble she?" Oxy turned away, ready to leave.

"Ah talk to her aunty and she tell me to talk to you 'bout it," Palance lied.

"Well talk to me some other time 'cause right now me hungry and me thirsty." Oxy's manner was dismissive, and he moved to put some space between himself and Palance, while reducing the distance between himself and lunch. Beady had waited for Oxy to join him near the food tables.

"Oxy, me notice Palance talking to you. Wha' he want?"

Oxy greeted Miss May and his aunt and was served his food, and both men began walking before Oxy said, "Nothin'; he no say nothin'."

They walked to the shade of a tree that was farthest from Palance, where they would be able to have reasonable conversations, and which they had to share with several men who were in various states of repose ranging from tranquil meditation to sleep. Among the men who were wide awake and full of conversation were Bonier and Plough, the most experienced cane cutters working that day. The men had been partnering since they were in their mid-twenties and their half-century birthdays were just behind them.

"Bonier, wha' you think of the progress so far? I think that we cutting at a damn good pace, right?" Beady asked.

"Well, boy, me have to agree with you, we should get through by four-thirty or five." Bonier's words were spoken in a husky voice that often caused second looks because it did not fit the tall, narrow fellow with prominent bones and not much meat. Bonier-than-Lucy was his proper nickname, for his mother's name was

Lucy, a skinny woman by any measure, and Bonier had even less meat than his mother.

"Plough, you agree with my estimation?" Bonier slapped his cutting partner on the shoulder to draw him into the conversation.

"Yeah, that a one good guess, me totally agree with you," Plough replied. Plough's name came from his feet. They were quite large and badly shaped. The quiet mock, because he was a big and tall man, was that he could stroll barefoot through an un-ploughed field and that stroll would have the same effect as a plough. He was also known for opting out of wearing shoes for all activities except weddings, funerals, and other church functions.

"Young fellas, me remember you from last crop time. How many crops you cut in you short life?" a self-assured Plough asked Beady and Oxy.

"Not as many as you two; this is about our fifth crop," Beady replied. He had a fertile mind and was always eager to absorb any information, any knowledge available from conversations with men like Bonier and Plough. Taking lunch under the tree with the proficient cutters was a deliberate move. "So you gentlemen have been cutting since the heyday of the sugar factory?"

"Yes, boy. Back in them days, we didn't just help out on Sundays; we had work every day when it was crop time. There was a ton ah work to do." And with a gesture to indicate the expanse, he said, "It seem like the whole island was covered with sugarcane back then."

"Yes, I can imagine. The island economy and culture was driven by King Sugar – everyone seemed to have a job related to sugar. From the cane cutters like you to the skilled laborers, craftsmen, engineers, chemists, and other trained professionals that were part of it. Now it is going to disappear with plenty displaced workers," a doleful Beady said.

Beady was an ardent advocate for the workingman and had been a keen student of labor issues since his days as a union hall juvenile. The men continued to talk as Beady and Oxy ate, and during what remained of the lunch break, Bonier and Plough were enthusiastically responsive, and eager to share their knowledge and experiences.

"It look like is time to start cut again," Beady said as he looked around at the other cutters, who had started to stir from their rest. He raised himself and headed back to work, while the young ones picked up wayward utensils.

The cutters went about their task with the same verve that was the highlight of their efforts in the morning. They continued to move together, swinging their arms, slashing and throwing the cut cane. Grunting and groaning were the only sounds heard from the cutters in Oxy and Beady's line; there was no conversation, except for Palance, who had positioned himself next to Oxy and was attempting to engage him.

"Me have one bad bone to pick with you, Oxy; you trying to avoid me but me go' talk to you before you lef' ya today. You not leaving until you talk to me." Palance was agitated by Oxy's earlier dismissal; he wanted a confrontation.

"Wha' you want to talk to him about? It so important to have you running you mouth and not minding you damn business, talk to him when you put down the machete, but in the meantime shut you damn mouth an' le' th' man work," Bonier said. "You can't be swinging th' damn machete and running you mouth chatting ignorance."

Chastised, Palance meekly bowed his head and focused on his work.

The work continued until late afternoon, at a rate that slowly decreased as the day progressed. At the end of the day, everyone, including the young ones, completed the collection and heaping of the cane for removal and transportation to the loco line. The island's locomotive system had a pickup station about one mile from Willie's grung, where the cane would be delivered for loading and transport to the sugar factory.

"Oxy, now is later and me still want to talk to you." Oxy and Beady were preparing to leave when Palance's aggressive talk made them stop. "You know me, and you know me no play. You need to forget making a move on me little cousin. Me aunty no want Tricia to talk to the likes of you."

Palance walked toward Oxy and stood close enough for the men to stare into each other's eyes, Palance with his best bad-man look and Oxy with a sardonic stare.

"Boy, get out me face with you stupidness. I talk to whoever I want, whenever I want. I'm a man who don't like confrontation, but your way of trying to intimidate people with your bad attitude and trying to over-awe them with your words work on the timid, but not on me. So get out of my face."

Without another word, Oxy ended the standoff by walking away with Beady.

CHAPTER EIGHT

The Court Date

The time had come for Oxy's court appearance, and Beady showed up as promised at the Little Court to support his partner. Little Court – the name used for the lower court – was located in Uptown, but the rambunctious vagabond types of Celadon ensured that the community was familiar with the location and workings of the court. Little Court was the place they would go to answer for minor offences like Oxy's missed child support payments, simple assault, theft of small amounts of money or objects of little value, and to sue a neighbor.

Beady worked as the foreman of a plumbing crew and as union shop steward at the public works. He worked Monday to Friday supervising one of the plumbing crews infamous for digging holes in the island's roads and leaving a mess. Because Beady loved Oxy like a brother, he had taken some time off to be in court to support his friend and planned to join his crew later that day.

Beady was a civic-minded person, and an ardent advocate for workers' rights. He was a member of the football team's management committee, an organizer at the union branch office in Celadon, and a delegate to the union conventions. The people he worked with and the people in his community considered him loyal, dependable, and a hard worker. He was a good man with a pleasant spirit, but he did not live an idyllic life, for it lacked the things he craved the most. The absence of children sometimes caused friction with Sister Ruth, his woman of long standing, and at times colored their union with sadness.

"Beady, me glad you come; you crew not out working today?" Oxy asked, happy to have his friend with him but worried about his absence from work.

"PW work rules are more like notions than actual rules," Beady joked. "No worry 'bout it. Nobody at public works missing me."

Earlier that day, Beady's woman had harangued him about the need to go to court. "Beady, the Lord would want you to be with your friend today," she had scolded mildly.

"Ruthie, don't tell me what to do," Beady had shouted, annoyed at what he considered audacious behavior. But as was always the case, he had quickly capitulated.

Ruth was a Christian woman who was slightly senior to Beady. Still shapely, she made every effort to hide that fact. She was a seamstress with better-than-average skills, and the money they made together afforded them the means for a comfortable place to live and a comfortable life. The couple had hooked up before Ruth found the Lord, and Ruth was unable to convince Beady to be a part of Brother James's flock. They'd never married, but nonetheless remained together. Ruth was familiar with the text regarding the perils of yoking with an unbeliever, but she loved Beady and saw only light in her communion with him. And her relationship with Beady was acceptable to her church, because Brother James's flock had the same attitude to church doctrine as did the workers at the public works to rules.

The souls that assembled on court days were the usual mixture of the summoned with their friends and families. Folks who had business with the court sat outside in the shade of a covered quadrangle surrounded by the court buildings. The court buildings were not much – a collection of worn early twentieth-century wooden structures with faded paint. The women wore colorful clothes: brightly colored dresses, pressed skirts, and pressed blouses. Some wore straw hats; others wore head-ties. The men in the crowd wore church clothes. The festive reds, greens, yellows, and blues of the women's clothing, though lively, did nothing to counter the gloom permeating the surroundings, weighing down the shoulders like a shroud of despair. Beady sat there for a short time, but found the mood dominated by an overwhelming, stifling sadness, so he left the shade of the quadrangle for the courtroom.

"Mister Jarvis," an imperious English magistrate, peering over his glasses, was saying when Beady walked in. He spoke to a fortyish man standing in the witness box.

"Yes sir, Your Worship," Mr. Jarvis replied, twirling his crushed hat with both hands. Mr. Jarvis had entered the court with his hat on, in breach of court rules and regulations, and had been rebuked severely by court authorities. He had taken his hat off quickly and crushed it to try to make it disappear.

"Do you have a barrister to represent you?" the magistrate asked haughtily.

"No, Your Worship," Mr. Jarvis replied humbly and with a most ambiguous smile.

"Mister Jarvis, the charge against you states that you stole two bars of carbolic soap, which were the property of Miss Millie Rose Martin. The charge states that she had placed the two bars of soap next to the washtub in her backyard before walking into her house, where she saw your conniving approach to her backyard through a window. Then she walked to her back door in time to witness your artful pickup and concealment of the soaps, and your exit from her property." The magistrate's statement was delivered in one breath with some vocal distress toward the end.

"How do you plead?" the magistrate continued after catching his breath.

"Not guilty, Your Worship." Mr. Jarvis stood erect, the posture of a proud man.

"Not guilty!" the astonished magistrate exclaimed.

"Yes, Your Worship, not guilty," Mr. Jarvis replied calmly. "Poor me," he added, assuming the demeanor of a victim. "Me?" He pointed his right thumb to the middle of his chest, and spoke in the manner of a person who had been put upon. "She sure is me? Is not me she see. Maybe the person she see a man that look like me, but oh Lord is not me she see."

"But you were seen taking the soap. Miss Mille Rose Martin's soaps went missing and they were found in your possession." The magistrate was apoplectic, and had more to say. "What do you mean you are not guilty? Miss Martin observed you stealing the soap and you had the soap in your possession when the police came to your house. How can you say that you are not guilty? I have never experienced anything like this. How can you stand there and just lie with such ease and calmness? Your behavior is maniacal." The magistrate used the most offensive term he could think of to describe the accused. But Mr. Jarvis was not done.

"Your Worship, I swear, a Sunday could fall on a Monday if I am guilty," he pleaded, clutching his hat with both hands beneath his chin, and his face transformed into that of a bewildered child.

The few spectators present in the courtroom were having a difficult time keeping straight faces because they saw exquisite humor in the exchange between the magistrate and Mr. Jarvis. They were familiar with the performance. To them it was always hilarious when the hypocrisy of a prim, proper, sporting, fair-play, honorable English gent clashed with the imperturbability of the Caribbean man. Beady left the court shaking his head and laughing out loud, a laugh that he sustained until he sat next to Oxy in the quadrangle.

"You shoulda hear wha' going on in deh, Oxy. One o' them expatriate English magistrate getting roughed up by a Mr. Jarvis. You shoulda been there; you would love it."

Oxy's laughter and knee slapping drew the attention of the people nearby, who turned to listen. "Yeah, Beady, a bunch a them come down here to help out the colony, that's what they claim, but is more than that," Oxy said. "An' me hear one a them get send back."

"For what? Wha' he do?" Beady asked, pleased that his partner was not distressed.

"Well, people say that he come down here with all good intentions, but fell in love with the rum." Oxy was in high spirits – he was always in high spirits when he told an unkind tale about an Englishman. "Beady, do you know that island rum is sold in England for ten times the amount that th' English importers pay for it? And their money is almost five times our money. Hey, I know why the sun never sets on the British Empire."

"Why?" Beady asked.

"Because God wouldn't trust an Englishman in the dark." The men shared a quick but hearty laugh. "Anyway here is the story 'bout the magistrate that get send home. He couldn't keep them royal hands off the Old Oak or the Cockspur and one night he was arrested behind the airport near that lover's lane. He was 'tone drunk and naked."

"Ah true?" Beady asked, then whistled.

"Yeah, the cheap rum beat him down," Oxy added.

The sounds of a woman's high-volume wailing startled Oxy and Beady. "Oh Lord, Father help me, me poor picknee, Father please, oh Lord, oh Lord."

The woman was prostrating herself near the entrance of the courtroom, where people fanned her with newspapers, paper bags, and hats. The prolonged, mournful, high-pitched cries and the commotion surrounding it generated a surge through the gathering, pulling everyone from their seats except Oxy, Beady, and a buxom mature lady who sat calmly reading her Bible.

"What exactly happen to she?" Oxy was calm but he raised his voice over the sound of the commotion, so the Bible reader could hear his question.

"She son get six months, so she decide to put on a show," the Bible reader said, looking over the rim of her glasses. "And ye mothers provoke not your children to wrath: but bring them up in the nurture and admonition of the Lord. She let him run wild and have his own way when he was a child, now she believe that she vagabond behavior will make her a good mother."

Oxy decided that he had heard enough of the mature lady's preaching and nodded a thank you. Turning to Beady, he asked, "Me ever tell you the story that I read about God and the young boy?"

"No," Beady replied.

"Well, this young boy asked God how long a million years were to him. 'A million years to me is just like a single second in your time,' God said. Then the young boy asked God what a million dollars was to him. 'A million dollars to me is just like a single penny to you,' God replied. Then the smart boy asked God, 'Could I have one of your pennies?' So God smiled and said 'Certainly, just give me a second.'"

"Goal!" Beady exclaimed joyfully. Then he pointed to a gray-haired, middle-aged man with a high, round stomach, who was walking toward them. "Eh, Oxy, look, one of them court officials coming over here."

"Mister George Stevens, Mister George Stevens!" the court official shouted as he approached.

"Present please, present please," Oxy stood up, waving his right hand for the benefit of the official.

"Your case has been rescheduled; the court will send you and your lawyer a notice with the new court date." The court official was a crusty fellow and had turned away before the last words left his mouth.

"Go easy," Oxy said to the official's back.

CHAPTER NINE

The Picnic

The church organized the annual picnic as a fundraiser, and the general public was invited. It had been well attended in prior years, and in anticipation of a good report at the next financial meeting, the church treasurer had hired two buses for the popular outing.

The picnickers gathered at the community school, where they would board the buses that would take them to the country for a day at the beach. The people on the island had always enjoyed unfettered access to all of its beaches and publicly owned lands, and they expected to have that right for all time. It was taken for granted, and most did not have a sense of what was about to happen. A drastic shift was underway in the island's economy, and the portents pointed to irreversible changes – the people of the community would soon lament the loss of unrestricted access to their unaltered beaches.

The Calvary Gospel Hall was a medium-sized church by the standard of the many churches that were scattered across Celadon, and it was the first of the American-style evangelical churches in the community, which had newly discovered Caribbean souls that needed to be saved. The newness of the church and its dynamic and freeform worship were popular with many Celadon residents, and that manner of worship was a direct challenge to the sustainability of the hegemony of the

Anglican, Catholic, Moravian, and Methodist denominations that had dominated the spiritual realm on the island since it was "colonized."

"Beady, Beady, what's hanging over you?" Oxy greeted his friend upon arriving at the schoolyard.

"Fry dumplings," Beady replied, as he organized his enamel food carrier and cricket gear: stumps, bats, and tennis balls. He moved the carrier, the two wickets (three stumps each), and the two bats from the path of hyperactive children who were running about.

"No, make fry dumpling stay 'til fritters come."

Both men laughed and touched fists. Beady wore a red cotton shirt with a white collar and a pattern of white diamonds and khaki short pants, in contrast to Oxy's peculiar attire.

"Oxy, so you decide to wear the team football jersey to the beach." Wearing the team uniform to the beach was against the rules, but Beady's tone was not confrontational, and his features were easy. He knew that the striped yellow and green football jersey and green shorts were the past season's uniform anyway, and that new colors would be available for the upcoming season.

"Promise me that if you see the young woman that you try to talk to that day by LickFoot Stanley, that you going to stay away from she please?" Beady's request was delivered with an edgy voice and an uneasy expression.

"Beady, tell me, how you know that she will be at this picnic?" Oxy asked with wild curiosity.

"Well, after that day outside LickFoot Stanley, I decided that if you didn't know who she was by the next time we get together there wouldn't be any point to not telling you, and since this is Ruthie and Sister Allen church picnic, I expect her to be here today," Beady said. The blaring horns of the arriving buses and the rising din together shortened Oxy and Beady's conversation, and prevented Oxy from hearing his sons' initial call.

"Daddy! Daddy! We are here." Oxy turned with a broad smile to see his two sons racing towards him.

"Uncle Beady! Uncle Beady!" After hugging their father, the boys turned to Beady and also hugged him. Beady then engaged the boys in playful conversation while Oxy had a chat with their mother.

Rachel was a reserved and intelligent young woman, with a complexion of light brown sugar. She had large eyes, a wide mouth, an afro, and the elegance of motherhood. She attracted second looks that morning, as she usually did, but not because of her arresting manner or because she was wearing a perfectly fitting green and yellow African print dress. Rachel – RayRay to Oxy and her family – paid her seamstress well, but it was easy to imagine the woman returning her money and paying Rachel instead to represent her work. On this day, she was attracting second looks because folks knew who she was, and knew the narrative of her long-ended relationship with Oxy.

"George, the boys were quite excited about this picnic and I brought them here expecting you to be an adult today," she said coolly. Her tone was stern but without malice when she added, "George, I'm trusting you with the boys, so please don't mess about."

"We should be back between five and five-thirty," Oxy replied, his sober and respectful manner indicating the esteem in which he held Rachel.

"I will be here when you return. See you then." Rachel did not dither, but walked briskly to her car and left.

Rachel had been Oxy's first earnest relationship. They were teenagers at the time and his hunger for the sweetness of love, the joy, and the bliss of a relationship like theirs was a revelation. From the very start, Oxy understood that Rachel had no patience for trifling ways. She was mature beyond her years, and it was clear to Oxy that he would not be able to dominate her. That appealed to him.

"Ox, your morals are weak, they are corrupt, and until you start living an upright life there is nothing there for you, so take that look off you face and forget RayRay," Beady rebuked gently as he observed his forlorn friend.

Oxy shook off Rachel, gathered his things, and headed to the bus, calling to the boys, "Ali! Malcolm! Help you uncle Beady with the cricket gear, we getting on the bus now."

"Which bus, Daddy?" Ali had gathered three stumps while Malcolm picked up the remaining three, and they also took a bat each.

"Let's get on the one behind." Oxy started to walk hurriedly in the direction of the bus he had indicated.

"Okay, Daddy." Both boys dashed toward the bus and were among its first passengers, despite spilling and having to recover their loads.

With all the bags, baskets, and other items required for a good day at the beach loaded, the picnickers filled the buses quickly and were off. The buses traveled to the southeast of the island, to a sandy beach along the shore of a deep-blue protected bay set between green hills and encircled by coconut trees, which was a common feature of beaches on the island.

The ride to the beach was not a long one, but it was a meandering journey through the countryside. The bus trip took the passengers through villages, around potholes, and over uneven roads with acute turns that tested the skills of the bus drivers and provided plenty of thrills for the passengers, including *uhhs* and *ahhs* from the children, before arriving at their destination to cheers.

"Boys, don't run off. Stay close to me; we need to find a spot and set up ourselves," Oxy called out as they left the bus. He and Beady quickly found a spot under a seaside grape tree, which they felt would provide everything they needed. Their first priority was shade, which the tree provided. The spot also met their second priority, which was location. It was fairly isolated, being far from the majority of the picnickers.

"Brother, me go look in on Ruthie, she is with the sisthren of the church choir," Beady announced after helping to organize their spot and patting Ali and Malcolm on their heads.

He walked past open spaces and a few solitary picnickers, on a leisurely stroll, taking in the scenery and saying hello to folks he saw on the way. He was leaving the sand to walk across well-worn and sun-deprived grass to reach the tree where the women of the choir were located when he greeted Ruth.

"Hello, Ruthie, you done set up yet? Oxy, Ali, and Malcolm down by the spot we pick out, a little ways off but we have good shade under a grape tree and plenty space," Beady said, pointing to the spot. "This place go' get dusty soon. The grass can't grow because them big trees block out the sunlight, and as soon as people walk around here one or two times the dust go' kick up." Beady frowned as he looked over the terrain.

"That's true, but we bring enough covering for the food, so the dust won't bother us," Ruth replied. "And besides, we in th' center of everything," she added.

Beady spent what he thought was an appropriate amount of time with the church ladies – mingling, greeting, answering questions, and offering suggestions on matters ranging from labor issues to church administration – before returning to his end of the beach. On his walk back, Beady took time to gaze at the water, and on returning to the spot he joined Oxy, who sat on the sand, and shared his thoughts with his friend.

"Oxy, you know what; I like to come to these picnics," Beady said. "I like that when we get here everything so fresh, clean, and natural. It's like the beach clean itself overnight in anticipation of its misuse in the morning. The sand is smooth, the water is crystal, the place undisturbed, and you can stand in the water and see the objects in the sand at the bottom. It even sound clean. Look at them waves, how they break so gently like they caressing the sand." The homage was interrupted by the boys kicking a toy football in and out of Beady's unspoiled water and in between the trees that were at the edge of powdery sand.

"Talk about disturbing the beach. Boys, boys, watch how far you kick the ball! I don't want you to kick the ball too far so you have to go chasing it where I can't see you, ok?" Oxy cautioned.

"Yes, Daddy," the boys replied as one, but their eyes never left the ball. Oxy didn't look at his sons while he was laying out this rule for kicking the ball. His supervising method was to let the boys have fun; he believed that they were old enough, and that continual observation was good enough, so continuous observation was unnecessary. He would talk to them often to verify that they were within hearing distance, even though he did not always look at them.

"Beady, you right about the beach early in the morning. It–" Oxy began.

"Wait! Where them people come from all of a sudden?" Beady interrupted, noticing the sudden appearance of picnickers near their tree. "Oxy," Beady went on, speaking softly. "Ruthie didn't tell me that Brother James have a program for the poor and destitute. You see who behind us."

Oxy noted Beady's wry smile before he spoke to the newcomers. "Rumgoat, ah who that with you?"

"Mountie and Buddy with me."

Buddy came into view – a perfect picture of what drinking chicken did to a man. His friend Mountie, who got his name from his favorite brand of rum, appeared beside him. The three men were regarded by those of exaggerated self-importance as lesser humans, but they had left the land of the wretched for at least one day. They were dressed in new clothes, wearing different colors of similarly patterned Bermuda shorts with red, yellow, and green t-shirts that appeared to have been pulled from the packaging that day.

"Me glad to see you fellas someplace other than the rum shop, and me hope that al' you nah have none rum hide-way, because Brother James will get vex," Beady said.

"At least Buddy can soak himself in the salt water – maybe that will help with the pellagra," Oxy said.

Rumgoat looked down at his friend's legs, at the signs of the ailment, before answering. "Me hope so too."

"Talk to you later," Beady said, and turned to Oxy, but Oxy wasn't done with the trio.

"But wait deh, fellas. Bata ha' sale on dem shit-mashers? All yo' wearing the same shoes. Look, one pair of them things is bad enough, but looking at three pairs at the same time is dismaying." The soles of shit-mashers were infamous for locking in stink, and Oxy was delighting in disparaging the cheap plastic footwear. When folks came together, outdoors, especially in an area traversed by domestic animals, any whiff of stink was followed by the question: "Who wearing shit-mashers?"

"Ok, I can't smell anything, so you all can stick around, 'cause you didn't step in nothin'." Oxy waved his hand with a smile to end the discussion, and Rumgoat, Mountie, and Buddy continued on their way.

"So what you think? You know you going to lose the job soon," Beady said, turning his attention to serious matters. "It is not long now until the deep water harbor open, and th' stevedore jobs gone. Oxy, a man like you, with your abilities, should be doing something other than manual labor. You have a brain, and you should use more brain and less hands."

Beady faced his friend directly, attempting to convey his concern for Oxy's employment deficit, but before they could get into it, Hosea and Serendipity walked by, Serendipity carrying a mysterious-looking crocus bag.

"Hey Oxy, wha' you say? What you and you partner up to?" Hosea greeted them and stopped to talk.

"Just taking it easy, watching people like you stroll along the beach," Oxy replied.

"We not strolling along the beach, we on a mission," Hosea countered.

"We going up the hill at the end of the beach to cut couple dagger log," Serendipity added.

"But wait, you all have implements, knife, or machete to cut them down?" Beady asked.

"Beady, you don't see who ah walking with?" Hosea said, with fake derision, the palms of his hands turned toward the sky, elbows at his waist, as if in prayer; he used his chin to point to Serendipity at his side. "He is a man of foresight."

"Me can't believe that he bring cutlass to the picnic. See you all later," Oxy said, before quickly adding, "Hold on, wha' you go do with the dagger log when the picnic done and we leave?"

"No worry 'bout that; we have a place to hide it 'til next year," Hosea replied.

"Ok, sir, later," Beady said, and as he attempted to return to their conversation about Oxy's job, Oxy interrupted.

"Hold on, Beady, look like some of th' young ladies from the church strolling down this way. I wonder if Tricia in the crowd." Oxy had heard what Beady said about his prospects for work, but the approaching young ladies were now his priority. Beady gave up.

"Le' me go share out some food to give Rumgoat and them. I'm sure that they could use some," Beady said, disappointed by Oxy's attitude.

Oxy shifted on the sand, moving closer to the water's edge. There was enough distance for the gentle waves to roll up onto the beach and not reach him, enough space for people to walk past without being too close. He was ready to chat up the young ladies.

Oxy called out to the group when they passed in front of him, and then spent a considerable amount of time quizzing them on trivialities about the church and the picnic, before getting to the whereabouts of Tricia. That was when a firebrand in a red swimsuit who looked a rebel – and with a demeanor that did not say proper church girl – confronted Oxy. She recited Oxy's associations, chapter and verse, with confidence, focusing on his encounters with women and his dubious position in the world. She made it clear how she felt about him, and how Tricia's aunt felt about him. She also made it clear that although she had not discussed him with Tricia herself, it was quite obvious how *she* would view him. It was a captivating monologue, and Miss Firebrand had the full attention of Oxy and her friends for the duration.

Oxy tried to say something at the end of her outburst, but could only muster one incomprehensible syllable. That was rare for Oxy, to be unable to find words; he was beaten down.

"Good, you have nothin' to say, well that is what I want to hear from you – nothin'. Let's go." Miss Firebrand turned to her girlfriends and they merrily walked away.

"What was that about?" Beady had returned in time to hear the end of the exchange.

"I asked about Tricia and the young lady that you heard, cuss me off."

"Hmmm," Beady looked around. "Where are the boys?"

"Malcolm! Ali!" Oxy called. There was no reply, and the boys were not in sight.

"Damn! Beady, you go that way and me will go this way." Both men walked off with urgency, Oxy struggling to control his dread.

As Oxy walked along the beach, he peered into the trees on his left, scanned the water to his right, and called out his sons' names. He moved fast, catching up with and overtaking Miss Firebrand and her friends, stopping to ask them if they had seen Malcolm and Ali. Even Miss Firebrand recognized that he was in trouble and answered with appropriate concern, but in the negative. Oxy thanked the young ladies and continued his search. His consternation heightened the closer he got to the unoccupied end of the beach. There was no one to ask questions there. He was alone.

The beach was bounded by rocks, which sheltered the habitat of precious intertidal life. At the end of the beach, Oxy began to climb slowly over and around the rocks. He thought that maybe his boys had walked around the rocks to pull whelks, search for mussels and shaligo (blue crabs), or look at barnacles and periwinkle. A walk around the rocks was always fun when they went together. He went as far as he thought it made sense to go, looked around, looked up at the hill beyond the rocks, and took a futile look into the water splashing beneath the rocks, then headed back.

On his way back, Oxy felt his composure disintegrating and hoped that Beady had been successful with his search. The thought eased his mind and he held it for a while as he hurried along, still turning to the left and right, calling out his sons' names, but his heart sank when he returned to his picnic spot, where he had imagined that he might have seen his sons. The beach suddenly seemed very short; he was running out of land to search.

Oxy's distress was in stark contrast to the merriment of the picnickers on the beach, and he was grateful that they were occupied with their picnicking and not interested in chatting with him. For the first time in his life, he wanted to be anonymous. He continued walking with purpose, and was just past the midway point of the beach when he heard the boisterous laugh, and, turning his head in that direction, recognized the red shirt with white diamonds that Beady wore that day. He stood under an outsized tree, sharing a laugh with a friend. Oxy began to walk toward Beady, then stopped, dropped his arms to his sides, clenched his fists, and took a deep breath. Beady had always provided solace when he needed it, and he longed for good news from his friend now. As he got closer to the tree, he recognized Beady's woman Ruth and some of her sisthren in the church, and his friend met his eye.

"Beady," Oxy's call was weak.

"Hey Oxy, I found the boys," Beady was quick to reassure after noticing the worried look on Oxy's face. "They were right up here all the time, they alright. Ruthie saw them running along the beach kicking the football so she brought them here, and gave them some of her potato pudding."

Beady stepped up to his friend and placed a comforting hand on his shoulder.

"Thanks, brother. Where are they?" Oxy asked.

"Go around; they are on the other side of the tree."

The tree had a trunk so wide that from where they stood, its width completely blocked the view of folks on the far side. The tree was the only one of its kind near the beach, a giant when compared to the coconut, seaside grape, and manchineel trees that provided shade closest to the water. It also dwarfed the few dumms trees, daggers, and giant milkweeds, which were further from the water and closer to the ends of the beach.

Oxy walked around the tree and gasped at the scene of a smiling Tricia playing with his sons. They sat on a Mackintosh spread over patchy grass, and were happily playing a game of pick-up-stones.

"Hello, George," Ruth was the first person to notice him. "Seems like the boys are having a good time. I hope you were not too worried. Beady told me that you might have been when you called to them and they did not answer. Not to worry."

"Yes, for a little bit, you know how that is," Oxy said, then recognized his error immediately, realizing that his comment might prick Ruth, since she did not have children, and was not likely to know "how that is."

"Not to worry, all is well now. You want something to eat?" Ruth flashed him a nervous smile from where she stood at a table loaded with baskets and pans of food.

"No, but I will drink some of the best mauby made on the island," Oxy said. Although it was the truth, Oxy hoped that acknowledging that Ruth's mauby was the best would counteract his previous faux pas a little bit.

Oxy walked to the table, and his movement got the attention of Tricia, her aunt, and his sons. There was a break in the flow of the game, which gave Malcolm and Ali the opportunity to say hello to their father. Tricia's aunt nodded.

"Hello, George." A greeting, a sweet surprise from Tricia to wash away the remnants of his despair.

"Oxy, you all right?" Beady came around the tree to join Oxy at the table.

"I'm cool, ah having some of Ruth's mauby. You want some?"

Beady said yes, and Oxy took a deep breath, because yes would lengthen his stay under the tree, and drinking mauby with Beady would conceal his desire to sneak looks at Tricia. They took their drinks and sat in silence with their backs against the tree trunk, sipping the bittersweet drink (which was brewed from the bark of the mauby tree) while watching the boys play with Tricia, and reflecting on the wonder of it. When they were finished with their drinks, Oxy spoke to the boys.

"Malcolm and Ali, it is time to go back to our spot."

"Do we have time to finish this game? Shouldn't take long." Tricia asked the question without taking her eyes off the game or the boys.

"Sure, Tricia, not a problem." Oxy was happy; he was having a conversation with Tricia. Beady was the first to stand, and both men said their goodbyes to Sister Ruth and her friends while Tricia and the boys finished the game.

"Okay, we are done." Tricia stood up, and in the interest of peace Oxy quickly looked away. He did not want to stare, did not want to risk a confrontation with Tricia's aunt, not even a non-verbal skirmish, so he asked Ruth an idle question before turning his attention to his sons.

"Boys, please thank everyone for being so kind to you today. Thank you all for taking care of my boys."

Everyone acknowledged Oxy's expression of gratitude, as he tried to remember the last time he'd uttered such a heartfelt thank you. Malcolm and Ali said their goodbyes to Sister Ruth and Tricia, and both were hugged by the women before they joined their father and godfather for the walk back to their own picnic site. After returning to their spot, Beady and Oxy settled quickly on the sand, watching Malcolm and Ali playing in the water, and checking out the people who walked by.

"Hey Oxy, look, it seem like Hosea and Serendipity done build th' dagger log. I wonder how far they plan to go on that raft t'day."

Oxy followed Beady's gaze to where Hosea and Serendipity were paddling away from the shore. "They probably have line and hook for fishing too."

"Wait a minute, wha' they using for oar, hope is not th' cricket bats."

Both men squinted at Serendipity and Hosea, trying to ascertain what they were using as oars. It wasn't their bats; Beady confirmed that after he went to check on their gear. He collected the bats, the ball, and three stumps for one wicket, and then he assisted Malcolm and Ali with the setup for beach cricket.

Like flies to spilled molasses, as soon as the wicket was in place, players came from everywhere. There were minimal rules to the game. Anyone could play if he or she could run a very short distance, catch a tennis ball after one hop (one bounce), or stand in front of the wicket and hit the ball when it came near.

"Hey, Beady, look over deh." The rum men – Rumgoat, Mountie, and Buddy – were ready to play, a prospect that Oxy found amusing. His laugh, though audible, was not loud enough for them to hear.

The three men, ignoring the curiosity of the other players, had a discussion led by Mountie before they joined the game in earnest. Mountie was among a gang of wicket keepers – he knew that it was the quickest way to get his hands on the ball. The rest of the rum triumvirate were in fielding positions on the left and the right side facing the batsman, as close to him as it was safe to be.

It took four deliveries before Mountie caught a ball, which he tossed to Rumgoat, who walked to the bowler's end and produced a delivery fierce enough to hit the wicket and uproot two stumps. The dismissal of the batsman provided his cohort Buddy a chance at bat. While the wicket was being repaired, an impatient Buddy pulled the bat from the dismissed batsman, telling him to "gimme um," and quickly assumed his batting stance.

"Oxy, people claim that Rumgoat stop from school in junior three at age twelve, because he stay down three times, but this sharing the work move, it's damn smart for somebody who stop from school so early," Beady said. The rum gang had a great resource management plan: while most of the players were attempting to be batsman, bowler, and fielder, each of them performed only one of those tasks.

"Watch it, ball coming." Oxy, Beady, Malcolm, and Ali were on the water side of the improvised cricket field. They had chosen the most undesirable fielding positions to give them some space and allow the boys to field without having to dodge the bigger players. It wasn't long until Buddy hit a high looping ball their way, and with no competition, it was an easy catch for Beady, who dismissed the batsman and called to Malcolm.

"Malcolm, hurry up, take the bat."

Malcolm sprinted to the batting crease, all smiles, and took his batting stance. He managed to hit two deliveries before being dismissed, but the short time at bat didn't define his moment at the wicket – the smile on his face, and the faces of his brother, father, and godfather did.

The game continued into the dullness of late afternoon, when the stumps were pulled and preparations to leave the beach began. The picnickers were not yet part of an emerging throw-away culture, and leaving meant that they packed up everything they had brought with them to the beach, removed the garbage they had created, and worked to return the beach to the state in which they had found it. And except for the disturbed sand and some broken branches, they did.

Malcolm and Ali had a good time that day, and they let their dad and godfather know it. So did all the children who were lucky enough to be at the beach, to enjoy its attractions free of restraint. No one at the picnic could have known, then, that days like that, days of unfettered access, would not last, not with a booming tourism industry looming. Oxy and Beady were in the camp of forward thinkers regarding social mobility and progress, but were uncomfortable with the monetizing of land and sea to feed tourism. On that day, though, their hearts were not troubled by such concerns.

Oxy, Beady, Malcolm, and Ali managed to get onto the same bus that had brought them to the picnic; the boys wanted that. On the ride back, everyone was silent, meditative, tired; the reverse of the passengers, full of music and mirth, who had ridden to the beach that morning. Everyone was blue – a wonderful day had come to an end, and the knowledge that it would be a long time before a similar outing dampened their spirits.

It was a short time between when the buses arrived at the school and when they dispersed. The picnickers unloaded, said their goodbyes, and were gone in less than ten minutes. Even Oxy's hand-off of the boys to Rachel was brief; Malcolm and Ali were worn out.

"They had a good time." Rachel and Oxy spoke at the same time, her words a question and his a statement of fact.

"Yes, they did," he confirmed.

CHAPTER TEN
The Revival

"Oxy, no tell me that you going up to the tent revival. Me know that you nah ha' th' Lord in you heart, so wha' else up deh that you interested in?" Brap and Tortoise had just sat down on the Corner for an evening's raillery, though by evening's end they would have touched or crossed the lines of slander, libel, denigration, denunciation, and disparagement.

Oxy, who was dressed in his usual dapper fashion – gray dress pants; powder blue, long-sleeved cotton shirt, sleeves rolled up above the elbows; and black loafers (a bit bold for the occasion) – was their first target.

"Oxy, boy you clean tonight." Brap offered a genuine compliment.

"Brap, boy me think he ha' eye on some young woman, some Christian young lady, and there's the place that he'll get to see she," Tortoise speculated, then looked at his friend and laughed. Oxy stopped as Tortoise continued to talk to Brap, loud enough for Oxy to hear but as if he wasn't present. "Or, hold on, maybe he just going to check an' see who come out tonight. You know that a lot of the young ladies in there tonight will be fresh to the eyes of fellas like Oxy. Those are the kind of young ladies who, when they not home, are either at work, or school, or church, and not running around to be seen by adulterers. To fellas like

Oxy, those young ladies are crisp and new," Tortoise concluded his harangue.

"Like new money," Brap added.

That was when Oxy spoke up. "Fellas you need to shut up. Not everybody want to si' down 'pon steps all day and all night and mind people business." He paused. "But if you must know, me hear that the American preacher is on a healing crusade – he claim that he can make the blind see and make the cripple walk. If LickFoot Stanley go to this revival tonight and offer himself to this preacher, you fellas will have to call him Stanley after the reverend lay hands on him."

Oxy wasn't really bothered by the antics of Brap and Tortoise, and he eventually said a polite goodbye and left them to turn their attention to the next target.

As Oxy walked away from the Corner, Beady was getting ready to step out; he always enjoyed the theater of a tent revival and was expecting to be thoroughly entertained. Beady and Sister Ruth's house was not far from Swinger Pasture, close to the center of community life, just how Beady liked it.

Sister Ruth, who was near the end of her preparations to go as well, asked a curious thing. "Tyrone, are we going to walk up to the tent together?"

"What?" Beady's response was brusque. "What you asking me that for? I am going to the revival, but not with you, and I won't be expecting the same thing out of it that you believe that you going to get."

"Ok." Disheartened, Sister Ruth spoke softly. "I will be on my way; remember to lock and check everything, make sure that nobody can get in when we gone."

Her manner was unsettling to Beady, who knew that he'd been the one to cause her discomfort with his gruff behavior. Beady often struggled with his ambivalence about his childless relationship with Sister Ruth, and felt in the moments when he hurt her that he was damaged too.

"I will do that," he promised calmly. When she left, Beady began sorting the clothes he planned to wear, still troubled by his behavior, which made getting dressed a somber exercise.

Soon after leaving the house, Sister Ruth met Sister Allen and was delighted because company would expel Beady's rebuff from her thoughts. The friends strolled along in silence until they approached the Corner and shared an anecdote about its occupants. Both women wore regulation sisthren dresses: hem below the knees, sleeves below the elbows, and absolutely no neckline. However, the restrictions in dress did not preclude form, and the shapely figures of Sister Ruth and Sister Allen did come through.

"Good evening, sisthren," Tortoise said, as they walked into the light of the Corner.

"Oomph! Oomph! Oomph! Look at that thing," Brap whispered discreetly as the women moved away.

"Me hear you. Those are the kinds of bottoms that haunt a man; yes, and linger in yo' mind for days an' days," Tortoise agreed, the movement of his head indicating admiration. "That bottom need to be in some kinda hall of fame," he continued, eyes focused on Sister Allen. "Both ah them. I mus' admit that every time ah see she, I feel a little twitch and warmness in my stomach."

"Boy is not you alone," Brap replied. "Whether you are a sinner or a saint, you bound to wiggle."

The bewitched friends sat still and wrestled to free themselves from the charms of Sister Allen and Sister Ruth's devilish derrieres long after the women were beyond the light of the Corner.

The revival tent was located near the Uptown end of Swinger Pasture; it was the usual deep tan canvas, set up to accommodate three hundred worshipers. Beady, as an official of the community football team, had not been happy when the arrangements were made to erect the tent inside the park. With the forthcoming football season not far off, the tent restricted the amount of space available for training; plus, the garbage that was generated after each night's revival spilled onto the playing field, creating extra work during preparations for practice. Still, not wanting to miss any of the tent revival drama, he hurried after he left his house, and got to the Corner quickly. The sun had not long disappeared, and the remaining light would linger for a while.

"Beady, you partner Oxy not long pass, and the sisthren just pass by not long too," Brap said.

"She and Sister Allen, two sisthren to the cores," Tortoise added.

"You fellas chat too much, always having something to say, nothin' pass you," Beady responded. "Why ya'll don't join the union? We could certainly put your oratory skills to good use instead of wasting it ponging mêlée."

"Ah-right boss, you and you union." Sarcasm and a hint of defeat ended the exchange.

The rest of Beady's trip was without incident, and he arrived to a large crowd, which represented the curious, the doubters, the believers, the near believers, the Oxy types, those who were looking for that promised miracle, and a few – just a few – libertines. The preacher was present, and representing Brother James's church were Sister Ruth, Sister Allen, and the rest of the choir members, who wore sisthren regulation dresses and were seated close to an improvised pulpit. That section of the congregation was colorful, lively, and expectant of a visit from the Holy Spirit. The revival had a standard routine: it began with the singing of the choruses, then testimonies, the star preacher's sermon, two collections, and the evening would end with healing of the afflicted.

Beady stopped briefly to get a good look inside the tent, then walked on. The flaps were up, and the folks inside were singing a chorus. The folks outside had a clear view of the proceedings, but were not singing. The crowd outside was building fast; its size would surpass the faithful inside by the time the healing began.

Oxy was close by, searching for Tricia. He spotted her in the tent, near the back of the congregation, which was always good for an easy and unnoticed exit.

Oxy and Beady walked individually through the crowd along different paths, checking out who showed up, greeting some, having short conversations with others, and moving in slow arcs that eventually brought them together facing the pulpit.

"Oxy, been looking for you," Beady said when they met. "Them clowns on the corner let me know that you were here already."

There was a slight hesitation before Oxy responded to his friend, and it was a few extra seconds before he gave Beady his full attention. "Yeah, I passed by them jokers earlier too."

Beady had noticed the slight hesitation and saw the reason for it. "Ox, me warn you from that young girl already, me just have a bad feeling about you getting into any kind of relationship with she."

"But Beady, this might be the one." Oxy was not about to concede.

"She too young for you, man." Beady was unyielding.

"Beady, you ah cramp me style," Oxy replied with a steady look, unswayed. "That Englishman that I like to quote said: 'The only way to get rid of temptation is to yield to it.' I can resist everything but temptation."

Beady decided to let it go; his friend couldn't hear, so he changed the subject. "Oxy, since we in the park, I know you said that you go' hang up you football boots, but I think that we go' need you help this year down in the second division. We will need you experience in order to get back up."

The men had walked away from the activities under the tent, stopping near one of the royal Poinciana trees that decorated the park along the inside of the fence.

"Yeah, I will do that," Oxy replied. "I will work it so that I can come to practice."

"You know that with the pending disappearance of the stevedore jobs, I was thinking that I could use my union connections to get you into one of them factories up on the airport road," Beady offered. "If we can do that, and get you into one that is strictly eight to four, that should give you the time to go to practice and to play when the season start."

There wasn't much light, but they could see each other clearly enough in the shadows of the early evening, and Beady made a gesture that was meant to ask Oxy what he thought of the idea.

"That would work," Oxy answered. "Now let's walk back through the crowd, Beady. Me want to see who me can see."

Beady knew who Oxy wanted to see; nevertheless, he walked with his friend toward the tent. Their paths diverged as they got closer to the tent, since Oxy was not about to go on a speculative search, and Beady was not interested in his shenanigans. Beady found his own way through the crowd, his thoughts on the proceedings in the tent, and he remembered when someone called Pastor Morris Cerrullo had plundered the island a few years earlier.

The pastor had arrived with huge fanfare, and managed to convince the islanders that he had heavenly powers. He had adverts on the radio – there was not much TV at the time – announcements at Sunday services, posters in store windows, flyers glued onto lampposts, and all across the capital the ubiquitous loudspeakers strapped to cars announcing his coming with great flourish.

The multitudes on the first night of Pastor Cerrullo's show at the national stadium surpassed even the crowds at the island's premier event, a three-island triennial cricket tournament. That tournament drew throngs from neighboring islands that jammed the stadium. It lasted several days, which included public holidays sanctioned expressly for the tournament, and Pastor Cerrullo's revival topped that. What the islanders did not know was that Pastor Cerrullo had been convicted of fraud at a different time and in a different place.

The most memorable thing about that night was the rebirth – the coming out of the forgotten, the blind, the crippled, and even the terminally sick, people who had not been out of their homes or institutions since what seemed like forever. Many families and friends incurred considerable expense to transport loved ones to the stadium in order to hear the healing prayer of the good pastor that night. But in the end, the absolute lack of miracles, the abysmal performance of the good reverend, put doubt in the minds of many, although some were embarrassed to have been swindled and would state otherwise. There were no miracles, although a huge sum of the hard-earned money of farmers, fishermen, laborers, and the unemployed slipped into the pockets of Pastor Cerrullo. It took a little while for it to sink in, but even the true believers eventually realized that the fellow was a mountebank.

Beady had a difficult time believing that people would allow themselves to be duped a second time by another pastor, so he put it out of his mind as he spotted an official of the football team and walked over to greet the man and begin a conversation about team business.

CHAPTER ELEVEN

Contact

Oxy's evening did get better, just as he'd hoped. The young ladies on the back benches, including Tricia, had made their move, and were now moving about outside. Although Tricia was with girlfriends, in the shelter of an ecclesiastical community of young ladies who wore similar dark skirts, subdued blouses, and church hats, Oxy was an expert at sequestering and easily isolated her.

"I'm glad that you stopped to talk to me." He had read somewhere that good grammar gets the girl.

"That question you asked required a response," Tricia stated bluntly. The question that had separated Tricia from her safety in numbers had been: "How different would your life be if we were friends?" She was eager to respond, but Oxy spoke first.

"Tricia, I know that my transgressions are well documented, but promise that you will give me five minutes."

"I will not promise you anything. I won't be rude, but I will listen to you only until your words cease to interest me."

Damn, Oxy thought, *she is just like the erudite Rachel.*

"Five minutes is a lot of time, and since my time is valuable, and my friends are waiting on me, I will give you two. What do you have to say to me?"

"I am lovable and capable … stop laughing."

Tricia was bent over in open delight, believing that Oxy's pronouncement was one of the most hilarious she had ever heard.

"Okay, that was an own goal; I scored on myself," Oxy conceded.

Tricia's laugh was infectious, and Oxy began to laugh too, caught up in the moment.

"Let's kick off again," he said. "My inarticulate start aside, what I was attempting to say is that, it was not so long ago that my sign was legible and it clearly said 'I'm lovable and capable.'" Tricia had straightened up and stopped laughing, and Oxy continued. "We all come into the world with an ILAC sign, and the lucky ones make it to adulthood with their sign intact. I didn't, but I believe that getting to know you could ensure its restoration." Oxy grinned.

"George Stevens, I know of you. I have heard your story. It is the story of a person who lacks character and quality. And I've heard of the dubious episodes that define your life." Tricia was resolute, and looked directly at him when she spoke.

"That is good; I was worried that my come clean speech would run over my allotted time. Good that you already know my weaknesses," Oxy said.

"George, you don't *have* weaknesses, you define weakness."

Tricia was a well-rounded young woman with a sharp mind a splendid disposition who aimed to be a success in life. She was as alluring and as charming as her mother, Eva, who was well known in the community for her vivacious laugh and her ability to influence with her breezy personality. Eva was smart and beautiful, possessing two of the three things needed to elevate her beyond where most Celadonians ended up. But she lacked the most important one: the wherewithal to do so. It was a time when social class and distinction were a great force in people's lives. For Eva, it was a negative force, since the desired result of a society that rewards standing and rank is that those who claim prominence and privilege remain few. However, Tricia had decided early in her life that she would not be stymied like her mother, and her self-assurance informed everyone of her ambition.

Listening to Oxy, Tricia realized that he had something, but was at a loss to figure why a person who seemed so talented would be working as a stevedore and have such a wretched reputation with women, so she decided to ask.

"George, you are aware that I and everyone in this community know about the wreck that is your life?" Tricia stood still, absolutely still, arms folded below her breasts.

"Yes, I am aware," Oxy answered, an answer that was delayed because at the moment of her question, his fancy evolved to adoration, which caused his mind to wander.

"Tell me, what are you doing – or better yet, what are you attempting to do? Because here is how I see it, George. I'm a young woman, I'm a whole woman, and in fact I *am* loveable and capable, and I am being propositioned by the most affected man about. So tell me, George, what you are doing?"

Tricia continued to look directly into Oxy's eyes and as late evening turned into night he was enraptured.

"I am talking to you. I don't believe that I have said anything so far that can be construed as out of place or wrong. What I'm doing is talking to you." Oxy took half a breath. "However, I must apologize for my tiresome chatter that day when you passed Beady and I outside of LickFoot Stanley," he said, speaking with the confidence that had deserted him earlier.

"Yes, that totally ridiculous figure eight comment – that was just awful," Tricia said, with a hand gesture that complemented her words.

The couple continued to talk; they were away from the illumination from the tent, and without any other light, they were shadows, indistinguishable to fellow Celadonians. The sounds of activity from inside signaled that it was time for Tricia to return to the tent.

"George, it was an unusual conversation that we had. I believe I actually felt pity, apprehension, annoyance, and the joy of laughter. But this interlude must end; I need to get back to the tent." Tricia turned away and looked around, but her friends hadn't waited. She began a slow walk toward the tent, but then stopped, looked over her shoulder at Oxy, chuckled, and said, "Really, talking to you was not boring." Then she picked up the pace and disappeared.

Oxy softly sang a line from one of his favorite love songs to himself. "And I know you can, make a man, outta the soul that didn't have a goal." Then he heaved his chest and exhaled, a loud sigh, and, no longer having any interest in the activities of the revival, began to walk toward the outer edges of the crowd, searching out the folks who were least interested in the show. He found his cousin and greeted him in the Celadon way.

"OnefromTen?" Oxy said.

"Leaves naught," his cousin, real name Bradley, replied brightly.

Bradley was nicknamed OnefromTen because of his association with the West Indies Regiment. The Regiment was an artifact of the short-lived Federation of the British West Indies, a political union of ten English colonies. OnefromTen was a soldier in the Regiment and had served faithfully until it disbanded. The nickname was an oblique reference to the curious arithmetic of an esteemed leader who had used the withdrawal of one island, the largest in the Federation, to justify his own island's withdrawal from (and the subsequent breakup of) the union. After the Regiment disbanded, OnefromTen returned home with the skills, mentality, and bearing of a soldier. He had a brusque personality and Oxy often took him along when an abrupt and crusty demeanor was required on some of his more risky rendezvous.

"Family, me hear that Palance threaten you at Willie cutting," OnefromTen said. Oxy could not see him clearly in the dark but he imagined a tight look on his face.

"You want me to deal with he?" OnefromTen asked. They were far enough from the tent that the sound of traffic from the nearby street was louder than the sounds of the preaching.

"No bother with that, me can handle fools like Palance. His strength is that fooley people are intimidated by his fanciful reputation, but the boy have no substance." Oxy put his hand on OnefromTen's shoulder. "How things going with you? How is Ethlyn? They treating you right at that hotel?" Oxy's questions were asked quickly, and with genuine interest.

After returning from his post as soldier, OnefromTen had had problems landing a position, but his woman, Ethlyn, was employed as a civil servant and received a big enough pay packet to provide for a roof, food, and clothes for herself and her man. Oxy knew that OnefromTen had recently accepted a position as head of grounds security at a beach resort. The position had been created for him at the behest or prodding of the union politicians. Oxy was glad to catch up, for he had not seen OnefromTen since he'd accepted the position as watchman.

"Ethlyn alright, and them leave me alone at the hotel. The job too easy, so if you have something that you want me to help you with le' me know."

"Okay, family, me know how to get in touch with you."

Oxy slapped palms with his cousin before walking off toward the Corner. He decided to walk near the boundary of the pasture inside the fence. Although there were sounds from the nearby street, it was quieter near the boundary and he could think a little about what had occurred during his chat with Tricia. He remembered the short disconnect during the conversation, caused by the glow – that trick on the eyes that makes the one you are crazy about gleam. He recognized it because it had happened to him before, with Rachel. Oxy smiled as he remembered the feeling, remembered being overpowered by the haze that made Tricia the brightest and shiniest thing in the park that night. He was so deep in thought that it took three attempts, shouting as loud as they could, to get his attention.

"Oxy! Oxy! Hey, Oxy! What you doing walking by yourself in the dark, you alright?"

The shouts were from three youngsters who sat on a boulder on the outside of the fence. Oxy knew them; they were not bad boys, but their antics stretched the boundaries of acceptable behavior, and he was certain that they were either in the midst of or planning some mischief.

"Fitzy, Tato, and Everton, you all behaving? Not getting into any trouble?" Oxy slowed his pace but did not stop.

"Not getting into any trouble. Oxy, where you going? By the Corner?" Fitzy asked.

"Yah," Oxy affirmed. "But me hear that you all hop a truck yesterday, and the truck hit a bump in the road, and Everton fall off, bruise up he knee. But he feel shame, and he get up and run after the truck again. Now you boys know that hopping truck is a very dangerous thing, right? You boys need to stop that. And I hope Ruthlyn boil some bush for you, some maiden blush and dolly macaroni, which should take care of any bruising on the inside. Ah-right? See you all tomorrow."

Now by this time, Beady's conversation about the football team's predicament was well underway. He had found several more team officials, including the president, and they were joined by a few other interested individuals.

"Beady, what are we going to do exactly?" The questioner was aware that Beady was not the president of the club, but because of his trade union activism and his penchant for getting things done, he was often called upon to lead.

"Well, as it stands it looks like we going down to second division next season," Beady replied.

"But that is pure ignorance. We always know that they never want us in them league, but to just throw us out so!" an agitated fellow shouted.

"They really didn't throw us out, they just relegate us," someone else clarified in a much calmer voice.

"Same damn thing – what it comes down to is that they don't respect us," Mr. Agitated shouted again.

"You can say that again." Mr. Agitated had a seconder who was just as roused.

"Hold on, just hold on," Beady interjected. "The situation is this: for now we will be playing in the second division for the upcoming season; there isn't enough time to change that. However, we intend to take the matter to our constituency representative and one way or the other, we will be back up next season." Beady was forceful but steady and his delivery had the desired effect. With everyone's full attention, he continued. "What we need to do is maintain our dignity. Fellas, you need to remember there will always be a disparaging word or two directed at us and our community. We need to go play in the second division, operate under the rules of the football association, and show them that we are not who they want us to be."

Beady felt that this impromptu strategy session mimicked the meetings with his union workers, and he liked it.

"So what's this thing with the politician you talking about?" The query was from Carl, the secretary of the football club.

"It was a suggestion from Samson. Not long ago, he and some of his buddies ambushed me on my way to the market, and that was one of the many suggestions that they made." Beady smiled as he remembered the encounter. "Samson suggested that we talk to our parliamentary representative. Get him to assist us, which he should be able to do considering his position in the government."

"Yeah, I see his car park up in the area after hours often enough. I think that what he getting down here after dark should make him more than happy to assist us." Mr. Agitated was still agitated, and his remark elicited a collective groan from the assembled.

The activities inside the tent had intensified and the sounds of "amen," "hallelujah," and "praise the Lord!" were no longer merely wafting through the pasture but were now blaring into people's ears, causing Beady to end his meeting and move closer to the tent for a better view of the performance.

CHAPTER TWELVE
The Corner Again

Meanwhile, Oxy was not far from the Corner, walking in the dark, when he ran into Edwin, a very dark man noted for his complexion and bright teeth. Both men were moving without sound and literally bounced off each other.

"Oxy, ah you that?" Edwin asked with a chuckle.

Oxy responded with, "How you know is me?"

"Oxy, me can spot you anywhere, anytime," Edwin replied.

"Hey, man, you give up on the preaching?" Oxy was still feeling good and was in a joyful mood. It was not a tryst, but his conversation with Tricia had felt like it. In another circumstance, he would have ended the exchange with Edwin after the opening greeting, but it was a special night, so he decided to be generous with his affability.

"Not really, but you know that me ah work on the new hotel 'round south an' me get up real early to catch me transport," Edwin said.

"You a mason, right?" Oxy asked, surprised that the sliver of information was stored in his head. Edwin was an 'A' class mason, and his skills afforded him elite status as a top mason island-wide. They continued on, chatting affably, until they entered the circle of light at the Corner.

"Oxy, I see you friendly with Radioface. Where you find he?" Tortoise shouted his question, and then began to speak to Brap softly.

Edwin had been nicknamed Radioface because his childhood friends thought his face resembled that of a radio. The children of parents who owned radios spent a considerable amount of time looking at, and listening to, their radios, and their imaginations had taken flight. The classic Blaupunkt and Grundig radios, with ivory select keys for medium- and shortwave stations, were the centerpiece of the home — except for a short period early in the year when elaborate schemes were developed to conceal them from the constable who collected radio license fees.

"Brap, you know 'bout Edwin?" Tortoise asked his fellow bad-hat, keeping an eye on Oxy and Edwin's approach. The story he meant to tell was not for Edwin's ears.

"No, wha' 'bout Baa Baa." Brap never missed an opportunity to allude to a person's complexion, so he used Edwin's second nickname, taken from the black sheep of the English nursery rhyme.

"Well, he 'bout a year younger than me, so when me start me second year of confirmation class, his mother decided that it was time for he to start. As you know, he live three houses down from me, so his mother asks me take care of him. Boy, me never see anything like it. So, I get with the boy and bring me catechism."

"So you get with the boy and bring you catechism," Brap echoed impatiently.

"So I show him the first paragraph of the Apostles' Creed and ask him to read it. You know the one: 'I believe in God the Father Almighty, Creator of Heaven and Earth…' and he linger. Well, he didn't say nothin' or do nothin' and when I look at him I see the fear in his face. So I point to the word 'Almighty,' and ask him, 'What is that word?' Nothing. To the smaller word 'Heaven'; nothing. And then I put my finger on the word 'God'; nothing. I should have stopped there, but you know me. I point to the word 'the'; nothing, then finally the word 'he.' Then it hit me, the boy can't read – and all the while, I was thinking that he just self-conscious." Tortoise completed his story in a whisper.

"That was long time ago; me sure he can read now." Brap's statement was without cynicism and he didn't laugh.

"Wha'?" Tortoise said, surprised by Brap's open optimism, but he let it pass. "Nah, he still can't read, but he have a trade; he is one of the best masons on the island and he mak' good money, and besides, me know plenty people that can read, but no have no common sense."

Tortoise ended the discussion just before Edwin and Oxy drew near enough to hear. Edwin said a polite "Evenin'," and went on his way, but Oxy took a seat.

"Wilberforce!" Oxy had barely seated himself when he shouted at the young man, a promising footballer, who was on his way home.

"Me hear on the evening news the other night that you school team went unbeaten last year and they expect the same from them this year. How you all manage that?" Oxy did not wait for an answer before continuing, making a genuine effort to recruit the young man. "Now that you done with that come home, time to move on."

"Wilberforce, me see you the other night, you and you partner and them two young girls," Tortoise interrupted before the young man could respond.

"So wha'?" Wilberforce responded.

"So wha'? So you feel you is big man, walking home pretty girls and kissing them in the building over so. Yeah, somebody see you, nothing hide 'round here. Le' me explain–"

"Wilberforce, as I was saying," Oxy cut in, "we would really like you to come practice with us, come represent your community."

"Well, it is something that I am considering; I'll let you know soon." Wilberforce said sincerely, and continued walking.

"Abolitionist, don't consider; decide. Is time to come home," Brap said, using Wilberforce's nickname and adding his voice to the recruitment effort.

"Okay, man; hope to hear something positive from you soon," Oxy called, ignoring Brap and encouraged by Wilberforce's declaration.

Brap turned his attention to a man in his forties who was strolling past, looking about suspiciously like a fugitive and exhibiting the mannerisms of a good-for-nothing.

"Look at that rapscallion, why, he still walking around with his head held high. Me know he shame bag rupture long time, but his latest escapade take the cake," he said with distaste.

It was customary for the rapscallion in question to take things that he did not own. He walked around on Sunday mornings selling plucked chicken, when everyone knew that he did not own a henhouse. He had embarrassed his neighbors when the police constable had walked around their neighborhood hoisting pot covers in search of pork that he was accused of stealing. That was all bad, but pilfering from the church collection was the offense that most dismayed the community and made him universally despised.

"Dawg!" Brap accused, when he was within hearing distance.

"Dawg? He is not even a noun." Oxy was agitated when he saw the lowlife.

"Wha' you mean by that?" Brap asked, confused.

"He is nothing. You remember the school lessons 'bout parts of speech? We learn that 'a noun is the name of any person, animal, place, or thing.' Remember that?" Oxy said, his voice seething with anger.

"So what you saying exactly?" It was not clear to Brap, and his face told that story.

"I'm saying he neither a person, a place, an animal, nor a thing." Oxy's reply was brusque; the man put him off.

"So wha' he be, one interjection?" Brap finally got it.

"Yes, like 'aargh,'" Oxy answered.

"You hear 'bout wha' he say the last time he go court for thiefing a motorbike?" Oxy asked.

"How that go again?" Brap's face displayed his struggle to recall the incident.

"Wha' you mean, you don't remember?" Oxy asked, merely for effect, because he began to tell the story. "So he on the witness stand, and the magistrate ask, 'How do you plead, guilty or not guilty of stealing the motorbike,' and he say, 'Not guilty, Your Honor, me have that bike since it was a tricycle, yes sir, and I raise it to a bicycle and now it's a motorbike.'" There was restrained laughter from some on the Corner, but Oxy wasn't amused.

"You know wha' he should be?" Fluxy spoke up. Fluxy was second tier – he didn't sit on the steps; he stood near them, and he was not expected to join the banter unless specifically asked, but he believed that he had something to add so he broke the rule.

"Wha' he should be?" Oxy asked.

"He should be a target in a coconut shy, and everybody get a chance to throw." Fluxy scored points and hearty laughs from the crowd. His real name was Warren; he got his nickname because of his fondness, as a youngster, for eating not yet ripe or "fluxy" fruit. Fluxy dumms, fluxy mangos, and fluxy guavas – fluxies were his favorite.

"Good one, Fluxy, that would be retribution for his nasty ways. And let me add, 'a whip for the horse, a bridle for the ass, and rod for the fool's back.'" Oxy said, quoting Proverbs.

After the rapscallion had passed, there was a break in the joking and mockery until the people from the revival began heading home; and the first person to show up in the circle of the lamppost's light was Vernie, a particularly unpleasant human being.

"How many books, chapters, and verses you think they would have to go through to find something, some scripture to sanctify she?" Oxy scoffed. "Boy, me tell you, if she show up in heaven, when the archangel that guard the gate see she, he go' run to the gate, pull the chain 'cross it, put on the lock, and tell she, 'the boss say, go away.'"

"Yeah, that woman ha' too much spots. How many lambs they would have to sacrifice to get she as white as snow?" Tortoise added, and Oxy laughed.

"Tortoise, nobody have to sacrifice no lamb, Jesus already make that sacrifice with his blood for everybody. All she ha' to do is make him her Lord and savior. But that not going to happen," Oxy finished with a smile, then continued with a Vernie story. "You know, my partner, 'Tace, tell me this story: His mother give him fifty cents and a big enamel bowl, and sen' him to market to buy five pound of fish. But instead of heading straight to the fish market, he decided to go by way of Bayside; he wanted to walk along the beach, and take in the scenic view.

"Well, as fate would have it, he bounce up some friends swimming and frolicking, and decided to have some fun. Sun bright, no cloud in the sky, seawater clear and blue, a delightful Caribbean day; he couldn't resist. So he say to himself that he was going to stay for five minutes; next thing five minutes turn into half hour and half hour turn into an hour (not that he didn't know how to tell time, mind you, but watches were rare).

"So by this time, his mother knew that something wrong; he taking too long, so she decide to go look for him. It didn't take her long, because she found him where she expected, and without fanfare had him collect his things and follow she home. Me partner say that he started the low-humming-bawling, you know the one, where you only break to catch your breath, and you sound like a stuck car horn. Well, that was his shield because he know wha' he mother had in store for he as soon as they reach home.

"So they on their way home along the big gutter, onto Parliament Street, and the first people them meet was Scarvell and he daughter.

"'Me beg for he, me sure he sorry, all young boys troublesome,' the daughter pleaded for 'Tace.

"Scarvell stopped working on his horse and cart to ask for a reduction of the lashes that 'Tace might be due when he got home. 'Take off two,' he said. 'Le' he 'lone. Take it easy. You know how little boys botheration; give him a break,' Scarvell pleaded, and that give 'Tace hope.

"'Tace mother asked him to walk faster, her face was tight and she was determined to punish. She told him to be quiet, but the bawling got louder.

"'Wha he do? It can't be that bad; me beg off two,' Mr. Lynch said as the sorry little procession of two passed by where he stood under a calabash tree in his front yard making fish pots. 'Tace saw a glimmer of hope – four lashes gone so far. So they reach by the Mack's house, everybody was on the front step enjoying the early afternoon shade.

"'Lea, wha he do?' someone asked of 'Tace's mother, but Miss Lea did not answer. She was walking in the blazing sun, the concrete road was hot through her slippers, she was upset, the sun was in her eyes, her face was creased, she was squinting, and she was not talking.

"'Whatever he do, take it easy with he. Me ah beg for he, spare him this time,' Sister Mack said mournfully, and everyone on the steps nodded in agreement. Miss Lea ignored them all, except to say good afternoon to Blind Job, who sat in the early afternoon shade of his house, and he begged for sympathy too. 'Tace was feeling good – he kept his cry going though, thinking positively about the outcome of his little saga; and then he heard it, that horrible voice.

"'Bang he, them too rude an' own way, tar he tail, them too love Bayside.' It was the voice of Vernie being Vernie. Everyone else beg for he, begging off licks, trying to soften his mother heart, but not she, the woman just evil. You know to this day, 'Tace a grown man, still hold a grudge 'gainst she. He say he never tell she howdy since that day, and as a child, every night he prayed for pestilence and plagues to befall her, although he didn't know the true meaning of those words."

The crowd roared with full belly laughter at the end of Oxy's story. By then, Vernie had walked by across the street from the steps, not knowing that she was being discussed, and was a shadow at the edge of the circle of light, taking her dark mind down the dark road.

"So, how was the revival?" Tortoise asked, full of mischief. He was in the mood to be devilish after Oxy's vivid portrayal of Vernie. "The preacher make any cripple walk? I heard that is his specialty."

Oxy soapboxed instead of answering his questions. "Not that I could see. One thing I know for sure, is that what the people listened to in there tonight will turn to sad tidings, and the joker will leave with money in his pocket, and the people that he flimflam will wake up tomorrow with sorrow in their hearts."

"Stop talk 'bout that nuh, gimme the mike for a little bit," Brap grumbled, feeling left out of the conversation. He changed the topic, getting back in and taking control. "Hey, Oxy, me hear that Palance have it in for you. Me hear he confront you at Willie cutting."

"Nothing pass you, Brap? How come you know 'bout that?" Oxy's voice and face registered genuine surprise that Brap knew about his run-in with Palance.

"Me have me sources," Brap replied, pleased with himself. "Oxy, wha' you do to Palance mak' he hate you so?" he chuckled.

Tortoise rejoined the conversation laughing. "I believe is because Oxy flop he down country club."

I should explain the flop and tell you about the country club. Dance was central to most cultural activities on the island. In Celadon, competitions were popular, and the better dancers were afforded a bit of celebrity. The country club, located in Celadon, was the number one dance spot on the island, so rivalries that were resolved at the club enhanced the winner's standing. Unlike the flop of an artist or an entertainer whose performance does not merit applause or praise, in Celadon the "flop" was the humiliation piled upon the loser, the shattering of his pride, and was comparable to a "bang off," or severe beating.

"You know Palance poor boast, but do you know that he 'fraid jumbie?" Tortoise offered, turning the conversation from Brap.

"Nothin' go so, big man like he 'fraid jumbie!" Brap exclaimed. "You telling me that he nah realize that th' stories 'bout jumbie, soucouyant, and diablesse are just stories to frighten children?"

"Yah, he 'fraid jumbie," Tortoise insisted. "You know he house in the back, so he have to leave the road and walk through a dark alley to get to it? Well, people say that when he ha' to walk through the alley at night, he disturb the neighborhood an' wake up everybody with his loud singing. He sing hymns, from 'Nearer My God to Thee' to 'On Christ the Solid Rock I Stand,' and at the top of his voice too; he believe singing hymns will keep jumbie off he. Some people even say that he walk with one Sankey at night. Them say that he not only wake his neighbors, but his singing set off the dogs in the area, and the dogs keep up their raucous long after he fall asleep."

Tortoise was glad to diminish Palance a bit with his tale and he wanted to own the Corner that night, so he continued with more questions. "Oxy how them twin boys-for-you? They doing okay?" He asked the question with a rare seriousness but didn't wait for an answer. "Tell me, what about their mother, Rachel?" And again before Oxy could respond he continued. "Now that is class. That woman demands respect. I mean, you know some people, not a lot, are sobering. Like, around other people the brain works, but around her it's fully engaged, and you find yourself having intelligent conversations; suddenly the mind is clear, and she does not have to do anything."

"Tortoise, sounds like you in love with my sons' mother." Oxy laughed at the end of his statement, embarrassing Tortoise. After he stopped laughing, he added, "Don't feel no way, she has that effect on people, men and women alike."

As amused as he was by Tortoise's embarrassment, talk of Rachel and his sons brought on a habitual sadness. She was indeed a special person. Folks never referred to Rachel as merely pretty, but instead used words like elegant, graceful, and lovely to describe her. Her parents had migrated to England when they were young, and that was where she was born, but the family had moved back to Celadon by Rachel's early teenage years. Rachel and Oxy met at a time when everyone who knew Oxy still believed in him. He'd been full of promise, and the relationship between the two was encouraged. Rachel and Oxy were bright, a fact that was reflected in their good marks in school and their radiant personalities. A few had assigned weight to the fact that Rachel was christened on a Sunday while Oxy, being a bastard child, was christened on the busier Friday, but those people were fools who continued to hold on to a life and a time that had passed.

As often happens when the young are overpowered by the intensity of uncharted passion, their boys were conceived out of wedlock. The couple had not planned to start a family, but Rachel's pregnancy met with strong and effective support from her friends and her parents, who had metropolitan attitudes. They would not disown their child; they did not feel shame because she was unmarried and pregnant; and they did not entertain the silly notion of sending their daughter away out of humiliation and embarrassment.

After the birth of their sons and the breakup, Rachel went off to London to study education, leaving her boys in the care of her parents. It was about that same time that Oxy followed his mother to New York. When Rachel returned, though she was quite qualified, she met some resistance to her appointment at one of the island's better secondary schools for being an unwed mother. It was well into the twentieth century, but a large number of female teachers with the title "Miss" were denied the joys of childbearing and motherhood if they wanted to keep their jobs. But times were changing, and through her father and his parliamentary representative, a progressive and forceful man, Rachel was able to secure the teaching position. She was a woman too capable to be denied; and Oxy, who had frittered away his own potential, and any chance of a future with her, could not deny that for him, Rachel was the woman who touched him.

"Oxy, wha' happen to you, you drift away?" Tortoise teased, bringing Oxy back to the steps. He shook off the regrets and rejoined his friends.

People were flowing from the pasture now, and most of those who passed by were offered a "Goodnight, Miss Ruby," or a "Goodnight, Papa Jake," until the stream slowed to a trickle. About the last person to walk slowly into the light of the Corner was the very devout Mrs. Messiah.

"You know, I have mixed feelings about that woman. She puzzle me. She used to be such a nice woman; outgoing, friendly, and she actually lived the life, the life of somebody I consider a true Christian. But since she husband passed, she still nice, but she get preachy too, behaving like some ah them that just discover the Lord." Tortoise spoke softly; he did not want his voice to be heard beyond the steps.

"Tortoise, that is what you call an enigma," Oxy offered.

"An enig who?" Tortoise asked.

Professor Oxy answered, "A person of puzzling or contradictory character," then continued, "Didn't she change church and gone to that church with that uptight preacher? He must ah tell she that if she too nice and not preach to people, the Lord go mak' the devil do wha' he want with she."

"Yah, that man so uptight, I wouldn't put that pass he." Mrs. Messiah was beyond the light when Tortoise finished the conversation, and Oxy stood and dusted the back of his pants.

"Fellas, it getting late; I'm going to split." Oxy had hoped to catch up with Tricia on her way home, but realizing that she must have taken another route, he went home happy that he had made first contact.

CHAPTER THIRTEEN
The Union Meeting

The day following the revival, Beady spent a few hours preparing for the union branch meeting. The parliamentary representative was scheduled to attend, and Beady planned to talk to him about the problem of the football team. The more he thought about asking the Honorable for his assistance, the more he liked the idea. The Honorable was a man of innovation who relished every opportunity to practice his oratory and persuasive skills. He had ascended to demigod status after convincing the organizers and other officials of the national beauty queen competition that it was time to elevate a dark-skinned woman to the throne.

Before that historic occasion, the light-skinned officials and the judges of the competition had an inclination to crown light-skinned young women as queen, so prior to the Honorable's intercession, there were always two queens reigning. There was the queen-for-upper-class and the queen-denied, the people's queen. The majority of attendees at the show believed the adjudicating was bogus, and felt strongly that in the time of Martin, Malcolm, Nkrumah, and Kenyatta, a black beauty queen was long past due.

The Honorable was way ahead of Martin and Malcolm, and he inveigled the organizers to do the right thing, to judge what was seen on the stage and not what was decided before the pageant. Eventually, the Honorable received his reward when an elegant black beauty, a country girl – despite the fact that country girls were not thought of highly – claimed the crown with her charm and grace. Her coronation was celebrated on parade day by jubilant crowds that lined the streets to get a glimpse of the future.

Beady hoped that the Honorable would be able to use his proven negotiating skills to maneuver the football association into bringing his team back into the top division, and had only positive thoughts on the matter as he headed to the union hall that evening. He was early, was enjoying his solitude, and had walked halfway to the union hall along a dimly lit Baker Street before someone called out to him. Walking in Celadon after nightfall had its challenges; the occasional lamppost light helped, but sometimes a flashlight was necessary.

"Beady, me hear that the big man go' talk tonight. Tell me, he go' talk 'bout wha' he go' do for people who go' lose them work when the deep water harbor done?"

Beady was walking in the opposite direction and across the road from the speaker. The road was narrow so they were not far apart, but at that moment, a car with too-bright headlights prevented Beady from seeing the person who had called him. The car and its lights moved him to the edge of the road, where he stood and spoke.

"Corduroy, is you that?" Beady asked. Corduroy was a fat fellow who got his nickname from the time when he owned a pair of brown corduroy pants. It was the consensus among those who judged such things that corduroys do not fit fat fellows well, and when he wore them he became a spectacle and was teased repeatedly.

"Yes, is me." The vehicle had passed and Beady could see the vague outline of Corduroy standing directly across from him.

"Yes, the big man will be at the meeting, and he will be talking about the harbor and other labor related issues," Beady said as he secured the load he carried.

"Me sure me will hear 'bout it tomorrow," Corduroy said, and turned to be on his way.

"Cord, you know you need to join the union and come to the meetings; you would fit right in," Beady called over his shoulder, continuing on his journey.

"Nah." Corduroy ended the conversation with a groan and walked on.

Beady arrived at his destination without another human encounter, but he had some difficulty trying to swat away mosquitoes while balancing his load as he passed pools of standing water at the side of the road. He made a mental note to talk to the Honorable about the standing water and ask him to get someone from the Central Board of Health to treat it and eliminate it as a breeding ground for the pests.

As Beady approached the union hall, he saw some members had congregated at the entrance and their presence boosted his already high spirits. They were early too.

"This place go' be busy tonight," Beady said softly, to himself. The early birds that had gathered near the door made way for him to open it and let them in. On this special night, with a rare appearance by the Honorable, the branch hall would be full.

The meeting started on time with all the usual formalities: welcomes, roll-call, and of course the liturgy. The chairman of the union branch addressed the membership about branch business, and then she introduced Beady, who gave the financial report. He'd arranged for this change in the agenda so he could meet the Honorable outside the hall upon his arrival. When he completed his financial report, Beady left the hall and walked down the front steps toward the street, where he greeted his primary school headmaster.

"Good evening, Mister Looby, how you doing this evening, sir?"

"I am doing very good, son. Tyrone, it looks like we have a full hall tonight. Is George's aunt inside?" the headmaster asked.

Beady stopped to give Headmaster Looby his full attention, and shook his hand as well. "Yes, she is comfortably seated; she is always on time."

"Good, I brought something for her; I will talk to you later." Headmaster Looby continued up to the landing, where he stood, caught his breath, then entered the hall.

Beady was not a habitual smoker, but the prospect of a "secret" meeting with the Honorable occasioned the light-up of a Plane cigarette. Plane was the local brand, produced at an industrial complex that was the home of several factories that manufactured, in addition to cigarettes, cooking oil, cornmeal, and arrowroot powder. The industrial complex was another triumph for the Honorable, the force behind its creation, who would, as often as he was able, secure positions there for his constituents.

Beady had just lit up when he saw the distinctive headlights of a car approaching. He identified them as the headlights of the very British Wolseley 6110 owned by the Honorable, so he dropped his cigarette, stepped on it, and sniffed himself, though he'd only managed three puffs before putting it out.

The Honorable stopped his car and leaned across the front seat to open the passenger side door. "Jump in."

Beady did, squirming around on the leather seat to get comfortable.

"I want to have a private conversation with you; let us drive around and talk," the Honorable was saying. "Let me get straight to the point. I want to offer you a job with the union."

Beady felt a jolt to his body, the accompanying shock constricting his vocal cords for a long time before he was able to respond. But when he did speak, his voice was clear. "I want to do that, I've wanted to do that for some time. Can you tell me what is required of me to get this job, and what exactly is the job that you are offering?"

"The job is the work of the trade union field officer, and as for the requirements, you have already met most of them." The

Honorable drove a quarter mile beyond the hall before he turned and drove to the top of a hill, where he turned off the paved road and parked in a meadow. From their vantage point, the men had a panoramic view of the night sky with few clouds, lit by a full moon and the sparse lights of the city across the harbor.

"Most of it?" Beady was genuinely baffled. He could not imagine what he had accomplished toward meeting the requirements for the job.

"Yes. You joined the union, have exhibited leadership skills, and have been elected as the shop steward on your job. You are active in your constituency branch, never miss a meeting, and you volunteer for branch committees. You have become known to members at headquarters and gained their respect and confidence." The Honorable did not look at Beady while he spoke, his gaze directed instead over the steering wheel of his car and into the night. "As for the particulars of the job, you will assist with job placement, prepare for collective bargaining and participate in negotiating sessions, become involved in grievance cases, do political work for the union, and, if a strike is necessary, ensure that it is carried out efficiently and effectively."

Beady nodded his head, acknowledging that the Honorable's explanation was precise and clear, reinforcing his reputation as an acclaimed public speaker. Beady did not say anything. He sat back in the seat and looked into the night across the harbor to the city. He had questions to ask, a lot of questions, but he figured it would need to wait for another time. He looked at his watch, thinking that it was time to get back to the meeting and pleased that his new-fashioned watch actually worked in the dark.

"Tyrone," the Honorable continued, "I must tell you that your real test will be to manage a successful strike. You will be assigned a shop which is likely to take strike action and you will be responsible for that." He turned to look at Beady to gauge his reaction and saw a young man in deep thought.

"Now, do not fret." The Honorable chuckled. He had recruited before, and attempted to alleviate Beady's apparent anxiety. "You will be educated and trained before we expect anything from you, and that won't be for some time."

The moon reappeared from behind a cloud that had covered it and it provided enough light for Beady to see and shake the outstretched hand of the Honorable.

"Well, son, let's get back to the hall," the Honorable said with a grin, pleased with the outcome of the meeting. He started his car, still grinning, and they headed back.

The chairman had managed the meeting in anticipation of Beady's chat with the Honorable. She sat at a table with a clear view of the steps to the front door of the hall, and when she saw the Honorable and Beady walking up the steps, she wrapped up her presentation to the membership and began her introduction of the guest of honor. The Honorable mounted the podium, then after scanning the hall and acknowledging a young – too young – woman in a red and white summer dress with a faint nod, he proceeded.

The Honorable spent his time at the podium motivating the membership. He spoke about the expected benefits of the deep water harbor, new jobs at the industrial complex, and the march toward a future where workers moved out of the fields and into offices and hotels. Once he'd delivered his fiery presentation, he visited with the branch leadership before heading home in the small hours of the morning after a social call on Miss Summer Dress.

CHAPTER FOURTEEN

The Union Job

"Beady, me hear that flour scarce, wha' th' union people ha' to do with that?"

"Flour scarce again!"

The question was from Blue and the exclamation from Liney, who, along with Beady, were just arriving at the beach for morning exercises and swimming. Members of the football team, players and administrators, gathered at the beach early on weekday mornings as part of pre-season training. Blue was a veteran halfback who felt that he needed to do a little extra in order to maintain his skills. Liney, a midfielder and Blue's cousin, got his name because of his exceptional play near the sidelines of the football field. Beady, Blue, and Liney were the last to arrive, and were late for the five o'clock start. Oxy and the rest of the team members were completing their stretches before starting their fifty-yard dashes, which preceded calisthenics and swimming.

The beach was located just west of Celadon on the south side of City Harbor. It was approximately one hundred and fifty yards of the island's ubiquitous sapphire water and fine ivory sand. The manchineel trees, which bordered the sand and ended at the start of a mangrove swamp, comprised the main flora; there were no coconut trees. The only blemish was the rusty barge that had been abandoned half in the water, half on the sand near the eastern end of the beach.

To the west, the beach ended at the start of a family estate that encompassed many acres and homes. To the east, a hill covered in trees shielded the beach from easterly winds. A narrow footpath over the hill provided one of three routes from the beach, a shortcut to Celadon. A second route was a hike over the rocks at the foot of the hill, along the water's edge, but with the difficulty of the hike and the myth of One Eye Rodney, it wasn't a popular route.

One Eye Rodney was purported to be a rogue shark that had lost an eye to the sling tip of a spear gun and lived in Rodney Hole, a narrow grotto that opened into the sea and recessed an unknown distance into the hillside. Unsurprisingly, there was neither written record nor eyewitness report from beachgoers, divers, or swimmers of a single encounter with Rodney.

Beady was soaring from his meeting with the Honorable and was eager to tell Oxy about it. He had tried and failed to locate the wayward Oxy the night before, so talking to him that morning was a priority.

"Beady, you late again buddy. I know that last night was your union meeting so I forgive you. Wha' happen last night?" Oxy and his teammates had returned to the starting line for their second fifty-yard dash. Beady joined in the exercises, lining up next to Oxy, who continued, "Beady, I understand that we might leave empty-handed if we stop off at the baker shop on our way home later, 'cause flour scarce again."

"But, Ox, you shouldn't understand that, you should know that – your job is to unload the flour boat when it come in," Beady reminded his friend with a smile.

"Yea, but you know that my work is play-play work, so I miss out on a lot of things." Oxy smiled too.

Beady leaned close and spoke in a whisper before the group began their second sprint. "Oxy, when we done exercising I want to tell you 'bout my meeting with the Honorable last night."

The questions and the conversations ceased until the completion of the sprints, after which everyone dashed, dived, ducked, or belly flopped into the water for a swim. Each person completed his individual swim routine, and then they all stood in waist-high water, forming an imperfect circle, and talked.

"Beady, is true flour really scarce?" Blue started in again. On the island, a shortage of flour was akin to a national emergency. Flour and rice were the staples of life in the community and the words "flour scarce" or "rice scarce" filled households with dread.

"So me know wha' go' happen now," Liney said. "Them shopkeepers go' start to marry them flour to goods that customers don't want or don't need."

"Yeah." Everyone present agreed, nodding their heads.

"But Beady, tell me that not 'gainst the law, that practice of marrying goods, forcing customers to buy goods that they don't want before they sell them the goods that they do need?" Oxy asked, annoyed that some shopkeepers would scheme to separate the broke from their last ha'penny.

"Oxy, you think that a man like Pusta Madre, in his narrow shop, go' respect that law?" Blue asked, referring to the storied shopkeeper with a bad attitude.

Pusta Madre's narrow shop could accommodate only two patrons at a time in the tight space between the entrance and the shop counter; any additional customers would stand on the steps outside to wait their turn. Pusta Madre would toss food items into the pan of his iron grocer's scale from the back of his shop or wherever he was standing, then pick the items off the counter or the floor without concern for health or hygiene when he missed the target. Though the narrow shop limited the distance of his tosses and restricted the number of missed attempts, his manner of operating was just rude.

"Well, you right about that. He and his fellow shopkeepers would certainly want to marry them flour with somethin' like oil meal, which seem to take up all the space in them shop and don't sell," Oxy conceded the point.

"I don't think that you fellas should worry about that just yet; it usually takes a week or two before things get real tight. A flour boat might show up soon," Beady said, attempting to end the speculation and provide reassurance. "The sun coming up; is time to get out of here," he continued, changing the direction of the conversation and moving out of the water.

It took five minutes for everyone to get dressed and leave. Beady and Oxy headed south, taking the third route from the beach; everyone else headed east to the shortcut over the hill. Beady had suggested the third route because he wanted extra time with Oxy to talk privately. Beady had achieved one of his life's goals and wanted his erratic friend to regard his achievement with all the seriousness it deserved.

They began walking at an even pace down the dirt road, stepping over furrows made by the runoff from the hillside when it rained, and avoiding intermittent clumps of devil grass and exposed rocks. The sun had not yet burned the morning dew from the grass at the side of the road, and the leaves of the nearby shrubbery had not returned to their diurnal rotation. Their flowers were still closed, the green of the leaves was pale, and they sagged for lack of sunshine, but Beady felt at ease; it was his favorite time of day.

The friends were looking ahead, scanning the side of the hill to their left for trees with ripe fruit and the meadow to their right that adjoined the mangrove swamp. Oxy was remembering rainy nights when the crab holes were inhospitable and a younger Oxy had taken part in torching parties with flambeaus (torches made of a bottle half filled with kerosene with a wick made from crocus sack), snatching the displaced crabs as they ran about looking for new homes. His face tightened as he reflected on the dissolute men who now, in dry weather, destroyed crab holes with pitchforks and pick axes, abandoning the finer points of torching. Oxy disliked the policy of altering or outright destroying of the landscape, and especially the altering of the shoreline and destruction of mangroves to make way for hotel construction.

"Last night, the Honorable offered me a job at the union headquarters." Beady paused to allow Oxy time to absorb and process what he said.

Beady's announcement pulled Oxy from thoughts of the crab holes at the edge of the swamp. His face relaxed when he heard the delight in Beady's voice, and he was ready to applaud his friend's good fortune.

"Yes, that is damn good news for you, brother," Oxy said with a double fist bump, and a little island shuffle to the left then to the right in celebration of his best friend's achievement. "Yes, brother, you on your way now. The problem is, do you think that they can handle you? You know some of them fellas down at that union hall not as righteous as you."

"Yeah, man, you know this union job was my dream, you know that, and I believe that I was meant for union work and won't have any difficulties with the unrighteous at headquarters." Beady's statement ended with a chuckle as the partners turned onto a paved road toward home.

"When you start? You go' give public works notice today?" Oxy asked.

On the paved road, they were immediately distracted by early morning pedestrians. Beady delayed his answer to say howdy to Mr. Tom, who was returning home after spending the early morning milking his cows at the paddock where they were kept. Mr. Tom rode his donkey ladies-style, supporting his milk saucepan, which he held with one hand on the beast of burden's back, just below the neck. Oxy and Beady were about to return to their conversation, but had to stand aside when Levi approached with a herd of goats.

"Levi! Wha' you doing, man? You take up the whole road and leaving goat shit everywhere," Oxy shouted. Oxy was Levi's mentor; they were neighbors and Levi's loyalty had been unwavering ever since Oxy had given Levi his outgrown bicycle.

"This is my herd, me will drive them how me want, no worry 'bout that." Levi knew that Oxy's shout was not in anger and he replied in kind, then returned his focus to his herd and shouted at them.

"See, see, see!" Levi shouted to keep the goats moving down the middle of the road and avoid the trenches on the side. Folks who owned livestock and had pets used specific expressions to ensure that the animals minded them. "See" was the expression used to direct goats, sheep, and pigs; "shoo" the expression to direct fowl; "come up" the expression to direct donkeys; and "hoosh," "mash," or "lie down" to direct dogs.

"Levi, I tell you all the time, that big brown ram kinda look like you. You sure is not you brother? And again, one of these mornings somebody going to hoosh dog 'pon you and scatter you goats, and wha' you go' do then?" Oxy chuckled and ended the banter with Levi before asking him for a favor. "By the way, you might not be able to do it this morning, but at least when you go move off later, after you herd finish they morning browsing, pick some lime for me. Okay, partner?"

Oxy was familiar with the pasture where Levi tied his goats for feeding – a place with brush, bush, weeds, small trees with plenty leaves, which his goats preferred over grass, and a grove of lime trees that outlined one side of the pasture.

"By the way, you eat any breakfast this morning?" Oxy started up the banter again. "Me know that sometimes you mama forget to share out for everybody 'cause is so many of you."

"Yeah, you treat me so bad, and you 'till want me to bring lime fo' you."

Oxy and Beady had a good laugh at that, then said goodbye to Levi and continued their discussion about the new job.

"Beady, I have a general idea, but I don't know exactly what the job is," Oxy said. "What exactly is you job; they tell you yet? And when you start? You go' give public works notice today?"

"Well, the Honorable said that after I receive the necessary training, I will assist with job placement, preparing for bargaining and negotiations, be involved in grievance cases, do political work for the union, and, if it's necessary, manage strikes." Beady walked on in silence, waiting for a response.

"That sound like a lot of duties, but it also sound like those are the responsibilities that you have been preparing yourself for. I agree with you, is you calling, you will do well." Oxy paused before adding, "Just no show them up too much."

Oxy's earnest response preceded an approving look at his friend.

"I am definitely the man for the job," Beady said, then quickly grabbed Oxy by the arm and pulled him from the path of an oncoming pickup. "Watch it! Look at that fool driving his pickup an' not minding he damn business."

"Hey, you fool, hold you side, man! Wha' the hell you doing!" Oxy's shout and his agitation got the driver's attention and his little Morris Minor pickup veered back to the center of the road.

"What the–!" Beady exclaimed, and he and Oxy continued their journey in silence until they drew near FatSlim's, where there was unusual bustle for midweek. "Oxy, why all that activity? It's not weekend; it is the middle of the week."

"Umm, hey, Beady, you know wha', is because of that man-o-war in the harbor; remember, the football team from the ship playing the island side tomorrow," Oxy said with a chuckle, having correctly figured the reason for the midweek bustle.

"Yes, yes." Beady understood. FatSlim was preparing for a rare daytime visit from the crew of a Royal Navy ship; he was a very accommodating businessman.

"Yeh, I guess it was the activity at FatSlim's that distracted the pickup driver. The man nearly run us off the road so he could get a look at the goings on in there."

Both men shook their heads in disbelief, and then Oxy spoke. "Beady, I am glad that you got the job you always wanted. You were meant for this job – the things that you do every day, organizing people, talking to people, giving them hope, authorizing them to stand firm, and advising defiance against circumstance. That is what you do."

Beady nodded his appreciation before speaking. "I want the job, you know that, but I have a slight doubt that it will work out. Not that I believe I am not capable, you know that too, but I will have to work with people that I don't know, in a high-pressure job and that is the downside."

"You know that you have my backing and that of all the people in the community that know you; that will never change. And the union, it's the perfect place to deliver your message of refusal to accept things as they are," Oxy said, looking over at his friend as they walked side by side.

The friends parted ways a short time after, with Beady saying thanks for the support and reminding Oxy that their absorbing chat had caused them to skip their planned visit to the bread shop. The two bumped fists before breaking away, Oxy walking up Johnny Hill to his aunt's while Beady continued on a direct path to his home.

CHAPTER FIFTEEN

The Talent Show

Oxy made his return to the stage on a Sunday, late afternoon, and immediately reestablished himself as a crowd favorite. He had made an impression during previous performances and was considered a rising star then. His personality, grace on stage, and ability to mimic American soul men Sam Cooke and Otis Redding had captivated the crowd, but he'd never followed up. Now he was back, a standout in a show where the competition for a spot in the lineup was fierce and the dread of being booed was all the motivation performers needed to do well.

Two topics dominated conversation in Celadon the day after the talent show. The first was Oxy's glorious return, especially his rendition of Sam Cooke's "A Change is Gonna Come," which he brought home. The second was various versions of an even more exciting spectacle, of which Oxy was also a part.

Brap, who had witnessed the spectacle, was eager to share his version of it. "You hear 'bout the rukshun up at the talent show?"

The crowd from the Corner had moved into the pasture to pass judgment on what they saw on the practice field.

"If you go' tell me, tell me." Tortoise was not keen on Brap's setup; he wanted him to just tell the story.

"I was there, so you know this is how it happen," Brap began. "Well, the best performance of the night was not from the girl-for-Tiny from Tinning Village, no, not even from Oxy who gave his best performance ever, no, it was from OnefromTen."

Brap paused and looked around at the crowd, expecting questions.

"OnefromTen was on the show? Didn't know he can sing," Tortoise said. He stood next to his seated friend, which meant that Brap had to look a long way up to his face.

"No, no, he was not performing on stage. Wha' happen is, that fool Palance was at the show. You know he go' show up if for nothing else than to show off. You also know he feel that he is a spook, a cool cat, and a saga boy. Yeah, yeah, I know they all mean the same thing but that's how Palance feel, he feel that he is all ah them in one." Brap paused so that the slower minds in the crowd could catch up before he continued. "The show was ending, The Playboys were playing some Booker T & the MGs, they had come on after The Teen Stars finished backing up that bow-foot girl that sing a good Marianne Faithful 'As Tears Go By,' don't remember she name, but that's when things got rowdy, shoving and pushing and misbehavior, and somebody push Palance against a wall where a nail catch he, and his trousers get tear. You know how he love he clothes, always think he clean, I don't know why because the boy can't dress, and when the nail catch he, he get vex and wanted to throw his tantrum on whoever."

"Brap, so wha' he had on?" Tortoise asked with a laugh.

"He was wearing a polka dot shirt, white background with red dots, puffy sleeves, white Dacron pants with white belt, and white loafers. You know that he not too tall, so the person that push him probably didn't even see him. So he in the place trying like a fool to look at his behind to get a look at the rip. He finally give up he stupidness and decided to walk outside just as I was heading out myself. As I reach outside, I was in time to see the fool approach Oxy, who had walk outside after his performance, and was rapping with Lou Ann, the limbo dancer; you know he love good-looking chicks." Brap paused briefly before continuing. He wanted his tale to soak in.

"Palance was well vex, and when a young man tried to tell him that he trousers tear, he turned to he and shouted, and I quote, 'Kiss me wah-rahee!' Oxy heard his cussing, turned, and chuckled when he see he tear-up trousers. I don't know why he had it in for Oxy but he fling one thump against the side of Oxy head after Oxy turned back to the chick. The blow stun Oxy, and he stagger little bit, but that didn't matter because guess who was picking up ticket at the function? OnefromTen. Boy, OnefromTen step in and hit Palance a cuff on the side of his head and the force and the surprise of the blow spread he out on the grass." Brap tried to demonstrate the cuff, and then a spread out Palance to an absorbed audience.

"But OnefromTen wasn't done yet; he pick him up like a rag dolly by the scruff of his neck, turn him around, an' hit him – whop! whop! – two backhand slap, then collar he, and tell he 'Me have this banging (a severe beat down) put up for you long time,' before chucking him back to the ground. A crowd was beginning to gather. Oxy had regained his composure and told OnefromTen that it was enough, but OnefromTen had to get in his last lick, so he grab Palance by his belt from behind and pulled it up to make him tip-toe, then OnefromTen toss he down a nearby slope." Brap paused to catch his breath, and to let the laughing subside before continuing.

"And you know after all that he didn't get enough 'cause he scramble up the slope in a rage and charge OnefromTen. Now, everyone know that Oxy and OnefromTen are cousins, but he also like a big brother to Oxy; and everyone also know that OnefromTen is a trained soldier from the West Indies Regiment. Palance know that too, but I guess he wanted brawta (a little extra), because he run at OnefromTen in a tantrum and got what he wanted. He got more when he run into a straight foot. The foot catch him in the chest; he fell on his back; and you know the boy vomit all over heself like one picknee."

The crowd surrounding Brap had grown, and the volume of the laughter had increased; it took some time before he could continue. "But is the police who save he arse; two constable show up and end the thing when OnefromTen was about to finish him off."

"You think that he going to behave himself since OnefromTen bang he so bad?" Tortoise asked after the crowd had settled down.

"Nah, he can't change," Brap replied.

CHAPTER SIXTEEN
Oxy's New Job

Beady got out of bed early after a late night. It had been several weeks since he'd started his new job, and he had made an impression on his new bosses. He had gotten home late from the union headquarters after some robust negotiations on a matter that was vital to him. He was tired, but had urgent news to deliver to his partner. Beady loved the morning, and always felt rejuvenated when he took an early morning walk through his front yard and gate, even when he didn't get enough sleep. The dew drops on the leaves of the hibiscus, canna, and red-green caladiums; the early morning bloom of the yellow and white angels trumpet; the fading smell of the lady of the night; and the presence of the other plants in his garden gave him that feeling of a new beginning.

Beady spent a few minutes in his front yard, putting together a bouquet of blue bells, pink and red hibiscus, purple iris, and some crocosmia, before heading to the home of his godmother, Lynita, who had decided to give up on the world and spend all her time indoors. As he walked slowly uphill, the early morning rays of the rising sun were at his back, just beginning to pierce the cover of the tamarind trees that featured on Johnny Hill. He took his time, stopping to trade greetings with folks on the way (no trip in Celadon was without a delay), discussing family, personal issues, the latest scuttlebutt, labor issues, and football.

Beady loved his godmother and, unlike most of her neighbors, understood why she might have decided to live as she did. Lynita had migrated to England as a gifted young woman, and she'd lived there for two years before becoming severely beaten down by the subtle prejudice and the not-so-subtle sexism of 1950s Leicester. Prior to leaving for England, Lynita had been a popular godmother. Godmothers were relevant and valued in Celadon then, and she had taken her vows as a godmother to heart. Goddy Lynita, apart from being a surrogate mother to her many godchildren, had been a woman of substance with many admirers. That was the woman for whom Beady had picked the flowers.

When Goddy Lynita's house was built, it was a standout house in Celadon. It was still a standout, based on its size, but it was rundown now. It had not been painted in a long time and a few of the boards on the side of the house needed replacing.

Goddy Lynita's family had owned and operated a thriving combination baker shop and grocery in better days. In Celadon, baker shops were rivaled only by rum shops in turning a profit. The baker shop had long been boarded up, and most of the family had passed or migrated, so maintenance of the house had been neglected.

As Beady left his godmother's house after dropping off the flowers, the tranquility of the early morning was suddenly replaced by chaos and Beady groaned. Every dog in Celadon was barking and Beady knew the cause.

"Doctor Knight in the area?" Beady asked no one in particular, certain the man was someplace close because of the volume and ferocity of the barking dogs. "It too early for Doctor Knight to be walking through the neighborhood."

"Yes, is he, he just gone through that alley," a chubby boy walking down the hill carrying a bottle of milk in each hand answered Beady's question.

Gawkers, onlookers, and giggling children usually came out when Dr. Knight was about, but Beady was not amused. "I hate that man; I don't know why the authorities don't do something about him."

"Hey, the bag that he ha' moving?" a jittery boy carrying a freshly pulled yard broom (a bundle of bush, bound tightly together) asked.

"Me no see," the chubby boy replied. Both youngsters stood in the middle of the street, taken in by the marvel that was Dr. Knight.

Dr. Knight was not a real doctor, although he insisted that everyone call him doctor. He was an overweight black man, not yet middle-aged but looking it. He dressed casually, if an outfit of khaki shorts, a worn tee or short-sleeved cotton shirt with missing buttons, and open sandals pass for casual. He plaited his goatee and carried a smooth, sturdy stick for protection from his snarling adversaries. It was a rumor, but the accepted story of Dr. Knight supposed that he earned the ire of all dogs by subjecting their fellow canines to unsanctioned experiments in search of new medicines.

"You, Boy-for-Miss Ivy; you, with the milk." Beady stood in the street and pointed to the chubby boy. "Carry home Miss Ivy milk, me sure that she want it scald before it spoil. And you, with the broom, you go home too, me sure that Miss James waiting on you to come sweep she yard."

The boys ran home as Beady expected them to, because it was a time when children responded to adults who were not their parents. After the boys left, Beady continued his stroll to the top of the hill through Gutly's neighborhood, issuing greetings as he went. The people of Celadon being early risers, he had a lot of greeting to do. When he entered Aunty's yard, he stood a moment and watched her go through her morning routine before greeting her. She was dressed in work clothes and it seemed to Beady that she had been up for hours, although there had been only half an hour of daylight.

"Good morning, Aunty. How are you doing and how is your day going so far?"

"Good morning, Tyrone." Aunty flashed him a smile, then, as if reading Beady's mind, said, "I have been up a while and so far it's a good day."

"Whe' Oxy?" Beady asked, slightly out of breath. He had crossed the last few yards to where Aunty stood at a trot after accidentally kicking the very short stump of a tree. He grimaced as he approached Aunty.

"Oh Lord, no hurt yourself! Me keep telling George to dig up that stump and he keep forgetting. You alright?" Aunty sucked her teeth, looking down at Beady's foot and then up at his face.

"I'm alright; it will pass soon," Beady said, still shaking his right leg. "Ummh, Oxy here?" he asked again.

"Tyrone, he 'round the back feeding the fowl. He late doing it; he should have done that long time ago." As she spoke, Aunty poured water into a washtub, for it was wash day. "Is the first time I see you since you get the big job at the union. They treating you good over there?"

"Yes, yes. Everybody treating me like I belong there; it will just take me some time to get use to the responsibilities and feel comfortable in the job. Yes, the people are just fine."

"Hey, partner, what you doing up here so early; I didn't expect you." Oxy had appeared with a grin, holding an empty chick feed container.

Beady chuckled and said, "I could hear you in the back saying 'chick chick come come.' Can't believe that you still say that. All you have to do is throw down the chick feed, and the fowl will come from wherever. Anyway, I have something to tell you, great news."

"Let me wash my hands and clean up and we can split." Oxy stepped away and out of sight to go clean up and Beady turned his attention back to Aunty.

"Aunty, since I'm going to tell Oxy soon, I don't see why I shouldn't tell you now. I got him a job at one of the factories. It is a good paying job and the best thing for him is that it is regular work, five days a week every week."

"Tyrone, that is good news, and should certainly make life easier for him. But how you just start and managed to get him a job so quick?" Aunty's question was talky-talk; she knew more about the machinations of the union and its politics than she let on. Beady answered anyway.

"It is something that I had asked about when they were running me down to take the job."

Oxy returned just then, ready to go and hastening the end of Beady's exchange with Aunty. "Beady, you ready?"

Oxy lead the way out of Aunty's yard, heading toward Mr. Reid's shop where they would purchase a workman's breakfast of bread, butter, cheese, and orange juice. They were halfway out of the yard when Oxy stopped to question a young boy who looked lost. No one in Celadon ever went from point A to point B directly.

"Aunty, the little boy-for-Miss Maynard come to you; he say he bring his grandmother box money (a neighborhood saving scheme with Aunty as the banker). I sen' him to you, an' we gone, see you later," Oxy called, then jogged to catch up with Beady who hadn't stopped.

That's when they heard the loud and piercing squeals of a pig. Beady sighed and looked about, attempting to locate its source.

"Damn, whe' that sound coming from, Oxy?" Beady grimaced.

"Is Palance, he altering some pig for Miss Freda." Oxy laughed loudly.

"Me can't believe that people still hire he for that." Beady was humorless, upset that despite his bad attitude, Palance was in demand for his abilities with a razor, and his skill in neutering pigs.

In addition to Levi's goats, Aunty's chickens, and Mr. Tom's milk cows, the residents of Celadon also raised pigs. For them, raising pigs was a low-investment, high-return proposition. They purchased a little sow piglet at minimal cost, raised it for even less, and then sold its offspring and eventually the grown sow or sows (if more than one was raised) for a decent profit. A twenty-dollar investment could return a thousand dollars after five years. Investment costs included boar's fee and cheap feed: oil meal, leftovers, peels, and discarded fruits and vegetables. Palance's altering skills ensured the viability of revenue from a boar's service fees.

It was a short walk to Mr. Reid's grocery shop, where both men ordered and Beady paid for their breakfast. Then they sat on the steps, where they had a view of the harbor and its early morning boat traffic, and could interact with anyone who passed by on their way to work or to Uptown.

"Squid, you go Bayside yesterday?" Oxy called out to Elroy James, who walked fast, heading down Johnny Hill. Elroy had demonstrated his swimming prowess as a preteen, and so the nickname Squid had replaced his given name. "Me hear that the people on the Nature Isle provision boat throw over plenty hogish yesterday. You get any? 'Cause me know that only the good swimmers can get to the boat."

The people of Celadon did wonderful things with the English language. One of their favorite constructs was to use the suffix *-ish* to create a describing word. Adding *-ish* to the word "hog," for example, described fruits that were slightly damaged but edible, drawing a comparison to hog food, which was damaged, rotten, and inedible. Oxy was referring to the hogish thrown overboard from the Nature Isle boat.

Nature Isle, an island of abundant greenery, fruits, and water, was a reliable source of bounty whenever the island on which Celadon was located, its complete opposite, was in the midst of one of its frequent droughts. Celadon was the home of many people, some originally from the neighboring Nature Isle, and all were part of the fabric of the community; except for a notable difference in intonation, Nature Islanders integrated nicely into Celadon life.

Tata, a native of the Nature Isle, owned a sewing machine and made a good living making curtains; replacing buttons on blouses and shirts; darning pants; and adjusting pant and skirt waists, pant cuffs, and skirt hems. He was also the provider of welcome services for new Nature Islanders arriving in Celadon. He helped them find a place to live, provided leads for jobs, and bestowed on newcomers a sense of belonging. Tata was well regarded, and he moved about with quick, light steps in his standard outfit of short pants, t-shirt, slippers, and bracelets. Tata was cousin to two sailors on the Nature Isle boat who were aware of his generosity and position in the community and eagerly provided hogish to his neighbors in appreciation.

Squid was a member of the elite group of swimmers who swam from Bayside to the boat, which moored midway between Bayside and the city docks. He swam at every opportunity, and the effect of the exercise on his physique was visible as he glided by Beady and Oxy.

"No, man, me no get no hogish. An' me in a hurry, me can't talk right now, the old man gone work and forget he lunch." Squid walked faster, swinging a white enamel food carrier. Oxy would have to wait for another day for a more detailed answer.

From the steps of the grocery, at the summit of Johnny Hill, Beady and Oxy looked at the boats and barges moored in the harbor and the large signs on the far side, could make out the north side of the city and the houses of the well-to-do on the hills beyond. Both men enjoyed the view, eating their bread and sipping their juice before getting to the reason for Beady's visit.

"I got you that job to work at the airport factories," Beady said, after a hearty swallow and swipe at his lips with the back of his left hand.

"Yes, that is good. Ahh…" Oxy paused, perplexed. "Factories?"

Oxy turned to look at Beady, who was halfway through a bite. Beady took time to slowly chew his food before explaining the job to Oxy.

"Yes, factories. You will be what they call a float. You will be trained and provided with the skills to work at all the factories.

The idea is that when someone is absent, you will be able to fill in and perform their duties. I really built you up for this job, not because you are my partner, and not because you need steady work, but because of your abilities."

"I never hear 'bout a job like that," Oxy said.

"You start next Monday; the hours are seven to three Monday through Friday. And something else: I'm close to getting a position for Tricia at one of the factories. She won't be on the shop floor but will work in one of them administrative jobs, but she will still be in the union, don't worry about that." Beady laughed. He was happy; it happened every time he helped a friend.

"Did she get the news from you already?" Oxy asked.

"Yes, I talk to her 'bout it two nights ago. She came by the house to bring some dress material to Ruth from her aunt and I told her then."

"Well, brother, that is great news. Finally some consistency. I will have a job with regular hours with regular pay," Oxy said.

Everything was suddenly different: the trees were blooming, all the houses were painted, the streets were clean, and the clothes worn by passersby were tidy and very bright or white. Oxy felt dizzy, unbalanced by the suddenly unfamiliar surroundings.

"However, I expect you to watch youself with Tricia."

At the heavy decree from Beady, the euphoria vanished. Oxy looked directly at his partner. "Okay, brother, I will behave myself. I will be ready next Monday and I will make this work. I have too many people depending on me right now."

"I would expect nothing less from you, my brother." Beady said, in a tone that put his friend at ease.

"Oxy and Beady, what you doing, sitting down on them steps so early in the morning? Yo' all sleep out?"

The questions were draped in a smirk and came from Victor, who was heading to Uptown with his younger brother. Victor, a plumber's apprentice with sticky fingers, was on his way to work, and his brother was on his way to secondary school. The latter was bright and articulate and, as a result, had been offered a robust education at an Uptown secondary school. The brothers were contraries but their deep affection for each other was unmistakable.

"Good morning, Victor, how are you today? You hear that? That is how sensible people greet each other first thing in the morning." Oxy's sarcasm hit the mark, and Victor's smirk disappeared. He pressed on. "I hear you taking you little brother to talkies with you now. Do you believe that taking him up there at night, especially when he have to go to school next day, make sense? And I know is Pit you go, for free, because the ticket man is you friend; I think that the twenty-five cents matinee on Friday afternoons is good enough for him. After all, even if he has to drill some bottles to make up the twenty-five cents to see the double feature, that easy enough."

Victor knew he was in trouble, so he did not stop to have a back-and-forth with Oxy and had gone ten yards by the time Oxy finished his reproach.

The island's principal cinema was sectioned, and the most inhospitable section, the one closest to the screen, was called Pit. Oxy's one visit to Pit had not been a pleasant experience. The seats were wooden benches that started at a neck strain distance from the screen and ended at a five-foot-high wall topped with six-inch nails that divided Pit from the rest of the cinema. Pit had unofficial seating assignments: patrons appropriated seats depending on where they lived in the city, and how disagreeable they could be. The most disagreeable got the best seats.

The seats were bug infested, and the more cantankerous patrons were known to do a number one on the concrete floor rather than leave in the middle of the show. On his one visit to Pit, Oxy had ruined almost-new trousers. His buddies had neglected to tell him to check his seat for used chewing gum, and to be wary of fools who released cowitch (*Mucuna pruriens*), to the distress of those who would develop painful rashes and scratch all night. Oxy detested Pit.

Victor and his younger brother had disappeared from sight and Oxy's attention was again on his conversation with Beady.

"Well, I thank you again, my brother, for getting me the job, and again I will be good at it."

"I'm going to head back up the road now; tell Aunty me gone."

Both men stood up, then dusted off the back of their pants in concert.

CHAPTER SEVENTEEN
Oxy and Tricia at Work

Oxy worked at his new job for two weeks before he was able to girl watch – his favorite pastime. At a place where seventy percent of the employees were female, it was an agonizing plight. Each day, he awoke early, prepared himself for work, cooked and ate porridge, and completed the short walk to the minibus that took him to work for a six o'clock start.

Once at the factory compound, he began work immediately. He took only a few minutes to swallow lunch, deciding to forego a real lunch break, and took no morning or afternoon recess. He was eager to learn his new job, and embraced his responsibilities. He participated in classroom training as well as practical skills training on the factory floor. Oxy believed that he had gotten the elusive break he had often groused about, and now that he had it, he strived for control as quickly as possible, and was willing to grimace and sacrifice his pleasures to prove that he deserved his friend's trust.

However, on workday ten, fate lent a hand. Production at the cigarette factory was behind schedule due to one of the island's frequent power outages, and Oxy was assigned there to provide extra hands. He entered the factory and was treading on excess material on his way to his destination when his shirt was tugged by a recent hire with nervous questions. The questioner had her back to the entrance, and when Oxy turned to face her, he saw

Tricia walk onto the factory floor. He was thrilled; her presence energized him, and even better, he had a reason to chat with her since he did not have a good answer for the new hire. There hadn't been many opportunities for Oxy to see Tricia at work; she arrived ninety minutes after he did and her workday ended a half-hour after his.

"Good morning, Miss Lewis." Tricia's simple greeting calmed the nervous new hire.

"Good morning, Miss Charles," Miss Lewis replied. The women's formal manner was normal in the workplace; workers always addressed each other using formal titles: mister for men, miss for unmarried women, and mistress for married women.

"I was about to come to the office, Miss Charles." Oxy joined the conversation. "Miss Lewis has some questions that you might be able to answer."

Oxy grinned, many teeth, and then he looked at Tricia in a manner not appropriate for the factory floor. Tricia saw the look, but she ignored it.

"Thank you, George, I think I know what the question is. That's why I am here; I will address it." A moment of silence passed between them, then a guilty smile, a look of contrition, and a blush. Tricia then turned her attention to Miss Lewis, and Oxy left to complete his assigned task. He was not long at it and on his way out, noticed that the women were still talking.

Emboldened by the ease of the earlier encounter with Tricia, Oxy decided to wait in the neighborhood of Tricia's office for an opportunity to talk when she returned. While he waited, he went through several scenarios for the conversation he planned to have with her, practicing a few opening lines. Some of the lines he considered he had heard in movies, some he had memorized from books, and a few were from his favorite love songs. But no, remembering the mess during their first encounter, he decided he would extemporize.

"Hi; what are you still doing here?" Tricia was startled to see him as she approached her office. She walked up to him, quickly covering the space that separated them, and looked him directly in the eye, challenging. "I thought you would have gone next door by now."

"I can see the twinkle," Oxy said.

"What are you talking about?" Tricia asked.

"Just to look into your eyes makes me wobbly."

Tricia's look of confusion was replaced by a stare. She stared, but there was a little smile, curled lips, and Oxy was not sure what it meant.

"I'm flawed." There was a pause, and a change in his demeanor, less bold. "The fact that I acknowledge that should give me some points, don't you think?"

"What do you want, George?" Keen to return to her duties, Tricia spoke hurriedly.

"We, meaning the football team, will be playing a pre-season match next Saturday – not this Saturday coming, the next one – and it would be nice if you attended." Oxy picked up on Tricia's impatience and spoke faster. "I know that you need to go back to work, but I have to tell you, we could use all the support we can get. I was told that you like to watch the games," he added, hoping to impress her with his knowledge of her fondness for football.

"I'll think about it. Goodbye," Tricia said, then turned and walked to her desk.

"Not goodbye, but see you," Oxy replied as he walked away, out of the building, across the parking lot, where he kicked gravel and said, "Shit, can't believe I said that. 'Not goodbye, but see you.' What an idiot."

Even so, soon after the first meeting at work, Oxy and Tricia began to spend time together. Oxy had become comfortable with the responsibilities of his job, and started to schedule timeouts that coincided with Tricia's breaks. The scant gatherings in the break room allowed for some space, quiet, and a chance to learn about each other.

When their meetings first began, they spent the time talking about work, and had lively and unguarded conversations regarding the dynamics of their jobs. But that soon changed, and they began to speak in hushed tones as they grew close, especially when the topic was Tricia's home life, and her relationship with her aunt. Oxy's life, as you know, was common knowledge, so the challenge for Tricia was to learn if the person transcended his history.

By the time the weekend of the football match approached, he had experienced the freedom of being himself when he was with her, and felt that he had a friend.

"George, we have been meeting often enough for me to have learned something." Tricia sat across from Oxy at one of the break room's sturdy varnished tables made from local wood by a local joiner. "It's a bit of a bromide, but I will say it anyway." She smiled. "You can't judge a book by its cover."

"What does that mean, what are you saying?" Oxy asked, and Tricia laughed.

"What, the bromide part, or the judge a book by its cover part?"

"All the parts." Oxy's cheerful response enhanced a breezy conversation, and Tricia prepared to clarify.

"Well, I am saying that there is more to you than your reputation. I'm saying that I like you; you are not bad company." She looked at Oxy, bit her lip, and waited for a response. Oxy was speechless, so she continued her clarification. "The other part of my statement – the use of the word bromide – was an attempt to describe the book by its cover expression, which is a tired expression. The expression lacks sincerity, and I don't want you to think that I am insincere."

Tricia stood, prepared to leave, and said goodbye before Oxy could respond. He sat alone for a while, processing what Tricia had said, and felt that he was at the start of a relationship.

"The fire catch, I need to pour oil on it," he said to himself.

CHAPTER EIGHTEEN

The Match

It was Saturday afternoon in Swinger Pasture: teeming, colorful, noisy. Bravo was selling his freshly parched peanuts wrapped in one-pound brown paper bags, which he carried in a large, clear, thick plastic bag slung over his left shoulder. Gobing – the duplicitous supporter, cynic, and incessant heckler – was present, walking the sidelines looking for contention, or for someone to hassle. Tina positioned her tray behind the south goal posts; it was loaded with mints, cigarettes, peanuts, chewing gum, Oh Henry, and dandy ball, with her sugar cakes and slice-up exposed to the dust and the dry grass that was everywhere. The afternoon was sunny, with no sign of rain. There hadn't been any sign of rain for many months, really, so the playing field was parched, brown, and cracked.

The home team was responsible for pitch preparation, and earlier in the day Vern, the team goalkeeper, had marked the field to regulation measurements with black oil instead of the standard white powdered chalk, which was not available. The goalposts were missing the regulation nets, but that omission was not a show-stopper. There were no stands or bleachers; instead the spectators stood on the sidelines, which they often ignored.

The visiting team was an aspiring club from the eastern end of the island. It was a non-league team, and their minibus had arrived early, giving them time to warm up before the spectators arrived. The Celadon team usually scheduled its pre-season matches *away*, against non-league teams from distant villages, which gave them the opportunity for a road trip and rare visits to the rural areas of the island. But there had been a mix-up, and so the Celadon team had asked their opponents to make the trip.

The referee, Mr. St. Clair, who was also the secretary of the football association, arrived from Uptown wearing a regulation black uniform and appointed a representative from each team to run the lines and assist him. The man was a tireless worker and devoted to the development of football, but neither his devotion nor his relationship with an admired Celadon schoolteacher eased the tension between the community and that particular referee.

"Ref, wha' you go' do today?" Gobing heckled, as the referee walked past him toward the center circle. Mr. St. Clair ignored the question. "Ah know you no love us, but you in we backyard today, so mak' de right calls."

Realizing that Mr. St. Clair would continue to ignore him, Gobing turned his attention to his next target, the team's top goal scorer.

"MostOutside, MostOutside!" Gobing walked over to the forward, shouting the nickname that was an implicit reference to shots on the goal that ended up outside the goalposts. It didn't matter to Gobing that enough of MostOutside's attempts were on target to make him the top goal scorer for the team.

"Boy, me no ha' no time for you ignorance," the right-winger replied, dismissing Gobing with a flick of his left hand.

"Me hope this year, you learn how to kick the ball in the goal."

The spectators in the vicinity of Gobing's irritable and sour voice shook their heads in disgust. To be the top goal scorer for the team was a special thing, but Gobing, a chronic disparager, did not appreciate that. Gobing was about to torment Oxy, but decided against it when he noticed a young woman approaching him.

Oxy was uniformed, and doing stretches when he saw an upside-down Tricia. He was looking backwards through his legs, while bending forward and touching the ground with the palms of his hands. He stood up and turned around to face a splendid Tricia, who wore a navy blue pleated skirt and a light-blue blouse with a puritan collar.

"Hello, Miss Charles, I am glad that you and your friends," Oxy acknowledged the two young women who were lingering nearby with exaggerated nods, "were able to show up. The team always plays better when our supporters are here." He looked into Tricia's eyes; he liked to do that, liked the good feeling caused by the twinkle in her eyes.

"George, there is no need for formality. We are not at work, and it is not necessary to refer to me as Miss Charles." Tricia's reply, and her disarming smile, encouraged him.

"Tricia, if you can stay after the game, I would like to have a talk with you. Is that okay?"

"If I do, we can."

Oxy welcomed Tricia's sassy response, and looked forward to having the talk; he felt that he'd never have enough time with her. But first, there was the game.

"Okay," he said, hearing a promise in her answer. "I got to split; later."

Oxy turned to leave, stopped, and then turned to face Tricia. "You know, you are what happen when a dream comes to life."

Oxy walked off to join his teammates on the field, not waiting for a response. Tricia was amused; she shook her head and rolled her eyes while her friends, who were now next to her, teased her about Oxy's lavish declaration.

The football match was dull, especially when compared with the antics on the sidelines. There were two early goals scored, one by each team, and the state of play after that was caution on both sides. The boring game gave the spectators, especially the mouthy ones, an opportunity to offer unflattering assessments of their team's performance.

"Ah wha' mak' ah you a play so? Me no trust ah you; ah you go' sell out the match," a young man standing behind the goal-post next to Tina's tray accused. He continued to heckle, loudly and rudely. "If you mak' any more goal score-yah today, you go have to take the long way home tonight."

Someone shouted at the young man. "Hey, boy! Boy!"

"Who you ah call boy?" the heckler fired back, turning to face a neatly dressed middle-aged gentleman wearing what could pass for church clothes. He was the team sponsor, and the one who had rebuked the youngster in defense of the team.

"Hear me, boy, me say stop heckle the goalkeeper; if you support the team, you support the team, and no come up in the pasture chatting one ton ah stupidness."

"Me ah one big man; me say wha' me like to anybody," the youngster said, then turned away from the gentleman.

"But you not acting like a big man; you acting like a little boy," the gentleman said wearily.

The youngster was quiet for a moment. When he spoke, it was in a voice and at a volume as if speaking to himself. "Me no know who you think you be, to tell me what to say."

The state of the game did not change much during the first half of the match, nor after the interval either; play continued well into the second half without a thrilling moment, until MostOutside volleyed from the top of the center circle past the visitors' astounded goalkeeper. Some spectators ran onto the pitch, some jumped, others pranced, and there was joyous shouting from the true supporters.

Gobing merely groaned. "Me no know wha' all you getting so excited about; dem no win yet," he pointed out scornfully.

The thrill of MostOutside's goal, ten minutes from the end of play, energized the spectators, and in the fading afternoon light, a defender from the visiting side kicked his legs from beneath him. The referee blew his whistle, play stopped, and MostOutside fell to the ground, indicating an injury to his knee. The smart spectators understood that MostOutside was merely wasting time – and they were of the same mind, wanting him to stay down for as long as possible. Voices were hushed, as the faithful anticipated the final whistle. The tension was thick all around, and then a cold voice pierced it.

"Haul 'e off, haul 'e off, if 'e foot bruk, haul 'e off the field and put 'e aside."

The callousness of Gobing's remark earned him vehement rebukes from everyone who heard it, but that did not put him off, and he continued heckling after MostOutside stood up and the game resumed, then ebbed to an unremarkable end. Most of the onlookers in the park were pleased with the result, but not Gobing, who began one of his tirades.

"You call that one win? The country team sell out the match, all you no play nothin' …and…" Gobing did not get far before an angry voice stifled his assault.

"Shut the fuck up! Wha' you be? With you, shit come out of the wrong end. The only one that … that … that I never hear you criticize and badmouth is Jesus Christ, and it's because you never meet 'e." Oxy walked off the pitch, headed for Gobing.

"Oxy, calm yourself; let somebody else 'buse he." A spectator put his arm around Oxy, who followed the advice and took a few deep breaths before speaking to Gobing.

"Disgusting live inside you," he said. "And if you open yo' mouth in the midst of joy, it would run away and hide." Oxy heaved his chest, took another deep breath. "You know, most of the people around here have good attitudes; a joke now and then, a little heckling, but we are a people of sunshine, clear skies, and blue sea; our personalities reflect that; but you, you, you are muddy."

Oxy glared at Gobing, waiting for the expected response, but what he heard instead was Tricia's call to him.

"George."

Her voice was the perfect antidote to Gobing's poison. He turned toward the voice, then walked over to Tricia, moving as close as was decent, and lightly touched her arm. If Gobing was responding, Oxy neither saw nor remembered him. It was an exhilarating experience, being in the presence of Tricia's delicate scent after ninety minutes of tussling with sweaty young men.

"Tricia, I'm glad that you were able to stay – let me remove my boots, put on my slippers – and we can talk." It was a fitful conversation, with Oxy speaking, then looking about. Finally, he called out to someone. "Patrick! Patrick, weh you be?"

Oxy was trying to retrieve his slippers, and he scanned the area nearby in search of the young man who kept them on game day. "Where is that boy with my slippers?" he asked himself; then he looked at Tricia. "Where are your friends?"

Patrick appeared, and Oxy stooped to untie laces and replace his football boots with his slippers. "Thanks, Patrick."

"They are on the other side close to the exit," Tricia answered, pointing out their location by moving her head in that direction as Oxy finished his business with Patrick.

"That is good," Oxy said as they walked in the direction of Tricia's friends. "And with a slow stroll, I will have a little chat time." Oxy presented his broadest smile and danced a little dance. "Are you going to give me a chance for more time with you, to learn more about you? I–"

"Hush," Tricia interrupted. "I talk to you at work; I talk to you whenever I see you away from work. Is that not enough?"

They were taking a slow stroll, opting to walk around the football field instead of across it. They walked a few steps side by side in silence before Tricia stopped, turned, and looked at Oxy. "On my part, I know you well enough. I am not giddy, but I am affected. I know you, the whole community knows you. You feature in many conversations and you are not always an endearing character. But I know enough to understand that we all have flaws, and I'd rather folks define me for all the things that I say and do, than for one act of bad judgment."

Tricia had decided that she was going to control the conversation that evening. "My aunt is a wonderful woman, but many in this community still refer to her by that name." She didn't have to say it; everyone in Celadon knew about Two-Pence-Ha'penny.

"One act of an angry young woman, and she was marked. But she is much more complicated than that. We are complicated beings and should be judged as a whole." She paused. "I'd like to paraphrase someone who reinforces my thoughts on judging people: To form correct views of individuals, we must regard them as forming parts of a whole, we must measure them by their relation to all the people around them, taking into account the conditions influencing the incidents in their lives."

Oxy opened his mouth to interrupt, but Tricia was not yet done.

"George, don't interrupt me." She said before a lengthy pause, giving Oxy time to think about what she had said.

"I like you, George," she admitted. "I sense that without the mask, you are inherently witty and creative. I can see a decent person beneath the cool cat persona."

Oxy didn't know how to feel, or what to say. His hand twitched but stayed at his side.

"I will give you a chance. I should run away from you, but presently my thoughts lack clarity, and I am seeing the things that make me feel good," Tricia concluded.

Still Oxy said nothing. Tricia waved her hand, indicating that it was okay for him to talk, but Oxy had no words. He was overwhelmed, but had wherewithal enough to raise his arms and lightly hold Tricia's upper arms, draw her close, and kiss her on her lips. She did not resist. When the heart acts, the body is a slave.

CHAPTER NINETEEN

Post Match

Oxy parted company with Tricia when they caught up to her two friends and the trio left on an errand. He continued on his way out of the pasture toward the Corner, which was an obligation after a football match. Upon reaching his destination, Oxy was about to sit when Tortoise noticed an unctuous passerby, and began. "Ah Poopy that?"

He motioned in Poopy's direction using his head, and then he said, "I don't even know why I call his name. I don't like that boy at all."

"Poopy," Brap called, but the self-important Poopy didn't respond, so he called out a second time. "Poopy, me no see you at the game at all?"

Poopy was the type of supporter who offered inane coaching tips from the sidelines during a match, and his prattle was an irritant to all who heard him.

"I was there, but I sat on the far side of the field with a couple other community leaders, Shinehead and Tully-for-Miss King; considering community challenges, you know, and coming up with ideas to combat them."

Neither Poopy nor the other two he named were community leaders. They just worked hard at giving the impression that they knew something. But everything Poopy said was out of context; people usually breathed a sigh of relief when he shut his mouth.

"That boy always come off buttery, like an ounce ah butter that warm up and leak out the wrapping paper, and drip over everything. Me always feel greasy when he 'round me." Tortoise shook his shoulders, faking a shiver, but Poopy had already moved on.

"Tort, do you know how he get that name Poopy?" Brap asked.

"No, how?"

"Well, they claim that one time, he tak' some Epsom salts for some ailment, and whoever give him th' thing was a novice, because they send him to school after he take it. Anyway, the salts start to work he during spelling for head. So Poopy spell his first word right, and was to move ahead of the two pupils who misspell it. So instead of moving ahead he hesitated, because there was gas and seepage. The teacher, trying to be nice, referred to him as Poopy, and it stick."

Brap's tale about the origin of the name Poopy, though improbable, was well received and the group had a good laugh.

"Oxy," Tortoise called, his tone authoritative, as if requiring Oxy to give account.

"Yes, sir," Oxy said, playing along.

"Me see you rapping with that nice girl-for-Eva, Two-Pence-Ha'penny niece. Oxy, that girl too good for you, and you not getting anywhere with she."

"You know something, Tortoise, there are certain things that you and you partner should keep out of, and that is one of them. So mind you business with that," Oxy said, so Tortoise and Brap dropped it.

"Hold on, hold on," Brap said. "Me see somebody coming down the road me want to ask a question."

And they were off again.

"Bambambam?" Brap called out to a young man when he was across the street from the steps. The young man was average looking, wearing clean work clothes, and his elbow locked a small bread basket on his hip.

"Come in ah me," the young baker replied.

"But Bambambam, me never hear of anybody selling bun at a football match," Brap said.

"I don't think that was a problem, Brap. It look like he sell off; he basket empty," Tortoise pointed out.

"Me hear you papers come through to go Canada – Montreal, Canada. Ah true?" Brap asked, ignoring Tortoise's interruption.

"Yes, ah true," Bambambam confirmed, then crossed the street and stood facing Brap.

"So you going baker school when you get up there? You go' learn to bake crêpes and so?" Tortoise teased.

"Crêpes? Tortoise wha' you talking 'bout?" Oxy interjected, laughing. "Crêpes? If he go to baking school is to improve his bread and bun baking skills, and learn to bake some fancy pastries in addition to bun-tart, butter roll, bread pudding, and potato pudding. Crêpes? Wha' you know 'bout crêpes?" he looked at Tortoise, shaking his head.

"Well whatever he go' study when he get there, at least he will get that sore-foot that he have fix; the gentian violet that he use nah work," Brap said, killing the conversation with Bambambam, who left, wounded by the sore-foot remark. Oxy had hoped that Tricia would pass by while he sat on the steps, but he decided to say goodbye and leave when Bambambam walked off.

After saying goodbye to Oxy following the kiss, Tricia and her friends had walked up to Mr. Lane's supermarket in search of ice cream, which was their tradition. Mr. Lane's was open from sunset to midnight on his Sabbath, and the light, glitter, and commerce of the supermarket's evening hours attracted various hucksters, including Miss Bell. Miss Bell churned out exotic flavors from her hand-cranked ice cream freezer, and her ice cream was celebrated by all except those who had never heard of or tasted it. The friends took a leisurely stroll home, so that by the time they approached the Corner their ice cream cones were gone.

Though devoted to the tease, there were certain people the men on the Corner considered out of bounds, and Tricia was one. Nevertheless, Brap and Tortoise spoke in whispers about her.

"That girl is as smart and beautiful as her mother, Eva. You know 'bout she?" Tortoise asked.

"Well, me hear people talk 'bout she," Brap replied.

"Brap, she was special. I'm sure she still is, but she live in New York now. When I was a little boy, well not so little, me use to walk up and down the road in front ah them house, to get a glimpse ah she. Anywhere I was going, wherever me parents sen' me, whatever errand, in whatever direction; I would find an excuse to walk in front ah them house. Ah not sure, but I believe she work me out, because one day she call me, and sen' me out on an errand to drop off something for she. Boy, it was the greatest day of my life then, but now, all I can remember 'bout that day is how good she smell, and how she brighten up th' place. That is a one special woman." Tortoise ended his homage with a groan, as Tricia and her friends were passing the steps.

"Good evening, Miss Charles," Tortoise and Brap said together.

"Good evening, Joel and Amos," Tricia replied, and then bit her lips to suppress a smile, breezing by without breaking stride. Her use of their given names was deliberate. She knew that it would cause snickering, chortling, cackling, and grunts of all kinds from the men on the Corner, because it would be the first time that most had heard Tortoise and Brap's real names.

"Amos? Which one is Joel?"

Someone laughed, and Tortoise looked over his shoulder, turned to the voice, and said, "You, boy, never, me say never, use them two name that you hear tonight, never."

Tortoise's firm rebuke was followed by only a brief silence before the ragging continued.

CHAPTER TWENTY
Tricia Chooses Oxy

"Tricia, them shilling loaf don't seem smaller to you?" Tricia's aunt stood in her kitchen-dining area facing a counter; she removed a loaf of bread from a brown paper bag, placed the bread on the breadboard, and searched for her breadknife.

"Tanti, were you saying something?" Tricia walked in from her bedroom and joined her aunt, who had moved to a small dining table. Together, they made final preparations before sitting down to Sunday breakfast.

"I was saying if you notice that th' shilling loaf getting smaller and smaller?" Sister Alice Allen had found her breadknife, and sliced the shilling loaf as she spoke.

"Yes, I noticed, and it seems like they using the same dough for sixpence loaf and the shilling."

They both had a good chuckle before sitting down to their breakfast.

"I hope that Mister Pilgrim not in th' mood to sing today," Sister Allen said.

"You and me, Tanti. It is first Sunday, and he's going to show up, sit in front, and make a fool of himself. Why does he behave like that? And why does he wear those clothes to church? He is the only man that I've ever seen in a coat with tails. The man just boast." Tricia smiled and shook her head.

"Since he young he go on so." Sister Allen stopped eating and looked up from her plate. "You ever see him at a funeral? He always stand at the highest point in the cemetery in his ridiculous outfit, raise the most hymns, and sing the loudest. Why would anyone wear tails to church and to a funeral unless he just want to show off?"

"And it's the same suit every time," Tricia added. "He is such a peacock, and he probably believes that his singing can raise the dead too." The women laughed happily. "Maybe that's why he don't have a woman, because he would be a hard man to live with."

Pleased that the reference to Mr. Pilgrim's lack of a female companion had offered a way in, Sister Allen said the thing that was on her mind. "Patricia, I understand that you kissed George in the pasture."

The laughter and warmth scampered from the room. There was a long silence. Staring. Pained faces.

"Are you going to answer me, Patricia?" her aunt asked.

Tricia placed her knife and fork on the table slowly, then drank some tea before answering. "That is partly true. There was kissing, but I did not kiss George; he kissed me. Tanti, it really is of no consequence who did the kissing, but the reporters should at least get it right." Tricia looked directly at her aunt. "I have developed a relationship with George."

She raised a hand to stop her aunt, who had opened her mouth to speak. "Let me finish. I am not his woman; we see each other at work, we talk whenever I see him away from work, and I enjoy the conversations. That is all the relationship is, and all, absolutely all, that has gone on between us for now."

Tricia raised both hands, fending off another attempted interruption. "Tanti, I am familiar with the list of George's shortcomings, his past relationships, and the number of children he's fathered. I know all that, everyone living in this community does. Tanti, I will not be swayed by a lecture from you regarding his prospects in life. What I want you, need you to do, what I am asking you to do is to give me the freedom to make a bad choice, and if disappointment is my due then I hope the Lord would recompense me according to my righteousness, according to the cleanness of my hands in his sight." Tricia tried to soften her words by quoting Psalms.

"Tanti, I love you, and you do know what, and how much you are to me, but I've been an adult for some time now," Tricia said with finality.

Sister Allen was bruised; she felt that Oxy was bad for her niece, and she loved Tricia enough to want to hold her close like she had when she was a child. But she also knew that Tricia was correct; she was an adult, and her bad choices were hers to make. Sister Allen just wished she could pass on the wisdom of time. While she was thinking, Tricia ended breakfast by getting up and collecting the dishes.

"Tanti, I think we should start getting ready for church. We need to be aware of the scribes in long clothes who desire to be held in high regard and take the best seats in the church."

"Yes, my child, and they only come to church once a month." Tricia had skilfully changed the subject, and Sister Allen acceded, but she was not done with the matter.

Tricia and her aunt's attitudes toward the relationship with Oxy had a common source in Eva's relationship with Lou. Their different perspectives demonstrated how differently people can see the same thing. Tricia was the daughter of Eva and Pat, but her father had died in a car crash before she was born — he'd been joy riding with friends in a Vauxhall Viva (a British car as secure as matchbox with wheels) — and with Pat gone, Lou was the only father Tricia had ever known. Eva and Lou had a bohemian relationship; he was an American expatriate, a contractor attached to the NASA tracking station located on the island, and a good match in Eva's eyes.

Their relationship began on Lou's first visit to one of the island's enchanting beaches, when he saw Eva walking with friends. What Lou saw was a lustrous young woman with gleaming teeth, a radiant smile, and a pleasant form, walking in slow motion among friends who walked at a normal pace and listened to her attentively. Eva's mother and father were not happy with the relationship, and were vocal about it. Her parents believed that Lou, being a temporary resident, was using Eva because she was beautiful, and would leave her heartbroken. They told her so. Eva, being a curious and vivacious young woman, was bold enough to venture from her protected existence, to embrace the freedom her relationship with Lou offered and expand her fertile mind.

Tricia had cloudy memories of the conflicts between her mother and her grandparents. She remembered her grandparents' determination to impose themselves on their daughter. She also remembered, vaguely, the wariness of Eva's friends; they seemed to think an outsider had stolen their Eva from them and they'd pulled away, which had made her mother sad.

Alice Allen's memory was clear: she remembered the folly in her little sister, and the disobedience that had created animus in their house. Sister Allen and her niece both saw in her blossoming relationship with Oxy parallels to Eva's experience, but for the aunt, those parallels were the folly and disobedience of a child, while for Tricia they were the restrictions and smothering of controlling guardians. We mortals often alter what we see with impressions from prior events; we see what experiences have influenced, and not what's before our eyes.

Sister Allen and her niece completed their preparations for church in silence, and did not say another word until they met Miss Roach, which was after they had walked half the short distance to church.

"Miss Roach, how you do?" Sister Allen asked.

"I'm doing okay this good Sunday morning, praise the Lord. Oh by the way, me just see Mister Pilgrim heading to church, an' he have on th' stupidness that he like to wear. Dear Lord, how you all manage that man inside your congregation? He is a vexation to the spirit."

Miss Roach's church was in the opposite direction, and though not of their congregation, she was familiar with the behavior of Mr. Pilgrim.

After parting ways with Miss Roach, the silence between Tricia and her aunt resumed until they arrived at church and were about to walk up the church steps. A middle-aged woman in a plain white knee-length dress and a headpiece that signaled the return of the cloche hat leaned into Sister Allen, whispered into her ear, then laughed, rolled her eyes, and turned her attention to another church member.

"Hello, Miss Romeo," the whisperer greeted another woman coming up the steps. "It's first Sunday and you know that church will be packed today. I just whisper in Sister Allen ear. I know how she 'love' when Brother Pilgrim come to church. He already inside and I'm sure he already take the best seat in the house."

Both women then walked up the church steps behind Tricia and her aunt and headed to their seats, giggling. Tricia and Sister Allen sat in their usual seats, and the church filled quickly. The choir members settled in and were ready to start the first chorus when Cece walked in. As soon as she crossed the threshold, all who had them went for their fans. Those who didn't prayed.

When Cece was present, everyone else performed the quick wind direction test: first, finger in mouth, then finger held up to wind. Folks always wanted to be upwind of Cece. The people sitting in the back of the church would be stuck for ninety minutes in her malodorous presence. The rustling of starched clothes and the sounds of shoe soles against the wooden floor grew loud as people moved about, attempting, in vain, to be free of Cece.

"First Sunday," Tricia murmured.

She and her aunt were lucky; Tricia sat near a window at the front of the church with her girlfriends, and Sister Allen sat among the sisthren of the choir, awaiting their cue to add a musical note to the proceedings.

"Ah-hem, ah-hem." Brother James was at the pulpit. When he cleared his throat to get everyone's attention, even the folks in the back settled down.

"First Sunday," Tricia repeated, and looked in the direction of the subsiding commotion.

"Brothers and sisters, I will not be giving the sermon that I prepared for the service today. Instead I will talk about brotherhood and providence. Acts 17:26 says: 'And hath made of one blood all nations of men for to dwell on all the face of the earth, and hath determined the times before appointed, and the bounds of their habitation.'

"First about providence and how we fit in. It is my understanding that when we came into the world, where we came into it, and the time we will spend in it was preordained. Brothers and sisters, we spend too many hours trying to satisfy our selfish desires. The Lord is our benefactor; we are here at his pleasure, yet we act as if we are more than a minor component of this great creation. Yes, brothers and sisters, we are minor players, but we still have a role to play under his direction. We might not understand why, but I do believe that he tests us every day. We are tested by the actions and behavior of our family and our neighbors. We have obstacles, and unpleasant things to overcome, but we must remain within the bounds of our habitation. Brothers and sisters, suffer your burdens, because there are no shortcuts. We must resist building towers directly to heaven. We must not attempt to scheme our way to the Promised Land; we have to get there by doing the right things every day of our lives."

Brother James paused for the congregation's amen before continuing. "And now, about brotherhood. All men, every nation of mankind, every man is our brother, every woman is our sister. Sometimes we forget. It is easy for us to forget where we came from and how we got here. Our daily lives are filled with drudgery and children, husbands, and wives to care for. During the twenty-four hours of a day, brothers, and sisters, our jobs at home and our jobs away from home fill every minute. The time we put aside for reflection we do not own, and we hardly get to use. But, brothers and sisters, I want you to, when you kneel down to say your prayers, think about someone other than yourself, someone who is poorer than you are, someone who has less than you have, someone who is alone. Brothers and sisters, I dare you, when you are kneeling, your hands clasped asking for consideration, I dare you to ask for someone who needs the Lord's assistance more than you do; someone like Cece."

Brother James paused and the sanctuary went from quiet to still. Even the women's fans were still, and then Brother James scanned the congregation from back to front, observing every face. He took his time, and everyone was enthralled.

"Sister Mason," Brother James's call to the organist pierced the stillness like the clash of cymbals, causing some in the congregation to jump from their seats, and Sister Mason began to play the intro to the next hymn on her program. Brother James and his congregation then quickly completed what was left of the order of service, bringing an early end to that Sunday's worship.

There was perceptible discord as Tricia and Sister Allen walked home. Tricia had decided that discussions about Oxy were done; her aunt believed otherwise.

CHAPTER TWENTY-ONE
Oxy Is Discharged

Oxy's court date had been rescheduled, he had been notified, and he presented himself on the appointed day, supported by his partner and his aunt, who sat uneasily in the waiting area. Oxy's party quietly observed the crowd, speculating about the nature of the transgressions that brought them to court. Beady participated in the guessing game for only a short time before he left the waiting area and, as he had promised himself, went inside to observe the court proceedings. On entering, he heard the beginning of a cross-examination.

"Mister Baptiste, I put it to you that you did not see Mister English take that bag of potatoes."

The lawyer putting it to Mr. Baptiste was a tall, light-skinned, athletic, London-educated man with a well-cut moustache and a perfectly trimmed goatee, dressed in a dark pinstriped suit. He had recently returned home to practice law and politics.

"You put it to me wha'? You can't put nothin' to me; you no ming deh. You weren't there, man; so you can't put nothin' to me." The agitated and glaring Mr. Baptiste unsettled the lawyer.

"Order! Order!" The magistrate was equally perturbed. "Mister Baptiste, your responsibility is to answer the barrister's questions and nothing else. No retort, no pontificating, if you please. Thank you."

It was a fair weather day, cool inside the courtroom, and there were seats available, so Beady took the rare opportunity to sit in the gallery and watch the proceedings, observing the theater of the case about an Englishman and a bag of potatoes.

Mr. Baptiste's story was that he saw Mr. English pick up and steal a bag of potatoes, which was part of a consignment being shipped by their employer. Apparently, while Mr. English was performing his duties near the potato bags, he saw an opportunity to bolt with one. He did not see Mr. Baptiste, who had noticed his shiftiness prior to his little caper and decided to keep a close watch on him.

Beady sat in the gallery for a short time, nodding and smiling, thoroughly entertained, as the polished lawyer struggled to break the witness; and as he made a noiseless exit from the courtroom, he promised himself that he would visit the court more often.

Oxy was having a quiet conversation with his aunt when Beady returned. Aunty was relating an experience she'd had the night before. She'd had a sense of foreboding and had put off her responsibilities for that day so she could be with her nephew. Aunty was dressed in somber clothing, in contrast to the usual cheerful island colors worn by the other women in the waiting area.

Oxy looked up at his friend's approach. "Beady, tell me, how it going in there? Anything interesting?"

"The usual bacchanal. Some Englishman thief a bag of potatoes on his job and now he hire a fancy local lawyer to joust with the gentleman who see he do it."

Aunty ignored Beady's report on the proceedings inside the court, but Oxy chuckled.

"Beady, ah always tell you about th' Englishman. In England, they amuse themselves mainly with religion and vice, so what you expect from this one?" Oxy laughed. He had been uneasy, but his spirit was always buoyed by a disparaging tale about an Englishman.

"George Stevens! George Stevens!" Oxy's name was being called by a court official, and his little party rose and headed into the tiny courtroom. It had a clean, unfinished wooden floor and electric fans suspended from a vaulted ceiling. The interior walls had fresh ivory enamel paint; the room was breezy and smelled like a library.

The magistrate, a dark, lanky looking gentleman, sat at a wide, polished mahogany table, a large notebook opened before him. He was a legend in Oxy's community, for he had overseen many disputes involving the citizens of Celadon.

"Are we ready?" he asked in a distinctive Caribbean accent not of the island.

"Sir, we are ready," the prosecutor responded.

Beady stood at the back of the courtroom where, given his position, he was the first to hear the uproar in the courtyard, and slipped out to investigate. Upon reaching the courtyard, he saw two women clawing at each other, the concept of the court and respect of the law lost on them.

"Lord, somebody put a hand," a matronly woman, part of the group that encircled the scratching women, pleaded. "Them women go' kill one another. Part them, somebody part them." She screamed.

The combatants were finally forced apart by two strong men, and it took all their strength to separate the scowling females.

"Kiss out me—" The younger of the two women, younger than her foe by a generation, was prevented from completing her instructions by the stern rebuke of an arriving constable.

"Miss, hush you mouth. Do you have business with the court?" He didn't wait for her to answer. "You cannot enter the court looking like that, miss; you have to go find some clothes, or at least a proper blouse."

The older woman was ahead on points when the fight was called, and the condition of the younger proved it. The older woman had shredded the younger woman's blouse, leaving her brassiere hanging by a single strap but miraculously still in place, while the older woman's corset proved suitable for a good fight. Along with the blouse and brassiere, the younger woman's fancy hairstyle was destroyed, and her hair combs were scattered all over the yard.

"Bolo, wha' cause this?" Beady asked his friend, a chubby young man with curly hair and a fair complexion.

The matter between the two women was of a son and former boyfriend. The younger woman had been a kept woman – kept by the son of the older woman, who had a court case that day.

"Them claim that the old lady son, Inspector Joseph, and–" Bolo did not finish his sentence because Beady interrupted.

"You mean the fire hydrant inspector?" Beady shook his head and muffled a laugh; he knew the inspector's story.

Some months before, the island had been in the midst of a marvelous mystery. Folks in the city, and neighborhoods close to it, were waking up to freshly painted fire hydrants. The hydrants were bright yellow instead of the traditional red, and no one could remember seeing them being painted. Folks would wake up in the morning, and there they were – bright yellow fire hydrants. The fact is, the hydrants were being refurbished. They had been rusting, unnoticed, and were obstructed by overgrowth. The mystery unfolded for weeks, feeding the chinwag, until Inspector Joseph was arrested for embezzlement, and the mystery solved. The inspector was accused of pocketing a portion of the funds designated for the hydrant clean up. He had been doing the work himself, under the cover of darkness; the law did not share his notion that since the work was completed, what he did was acceptable.

"Yes, he self, and his keep-woman come set obeah 'pon he, because he promise his wife to use the extra money to take her to Gloucestershire, England, on vacation. He wanted to visit his fire brigade college, and he didn't tell the keep-woman nothin' 'bout it. But you know, no loving mother go' allow any woman to put a curse on she son, so cussing start, and fighting break out," Bolo explained.

"But Bolo, how come you know so damn much 'bout the fire inspector business, eh? Anyway, it seem like the action done out here so I going back inside."

Beady was heading back inside the courtroom when he saw Oxy and Aunty leaving. Oxy had been granted a reprieve. Beady had known about it, since he was party to the negotiated settlement, which had been agreed to the night before. He had petitioned the union's important persons who were wired into the political and legal system to make a plea for a settlement. That type of arrangement was not uncommon, and the settlement kept Oxy out of jail but required that the pay from his new job would be the property of the court, and the court would have first claim. In other words, the court would deduct the child payments he owed from his weekly pay packet, and the remainder would go to him until his payments were up to date. Oxy was not unhappy with the decision because he'd always wanted to pay, and the weekly cost of child support was considered a joke. Folks literally joked about it, it was such a paltry sum.

"Beady, did you know about this deal and didn't tell me?" Oxy asked with a broad smile.

"Yes, I did, but I was sworn to secrecy, you understand." Beady's grin was just as wide.

"Aunty, let's go," Oxy said to his aunt. She was in better spirits, Oxy was relieved, and Beady satisfied. Although not deliberately, he had caused Aunty some pain, and he hated when that happened.

"Yes, let's go," she said. "Thank the Lord that this thing done."

CHAPTER TWENTY-TWO

Oxy's Transformation

Oxy basked in the glow of his most recent successes; he had gained some favor with Tricia, and that made him happy. He had managed to escape incarceration, and that made him happy. And having overcome that most difficult challenge, he felt that it was time to effect changes in his life. He had no ideals and no goals, he was not a teenager, and he finally realized that sauntering through life was not good enough. Sitting quietly in the fading light, he reran a recent reproof from his aunt.

"The tragedy of our lives is not in living above our ability, but in living below our capabilities." The borrowed credo was one Aunty's favorites.

Oxy sat on a tree stump positioned near the line where the landscape changed from sand to grass. He often sat on the stump when he wanted to organize his thoughts and try for an unruffled mind. The late afternoon peace and quiet of Bayside was ideal for that. The brown boobies making their final passes of the day, looking to swoop down and gulp one last fish, and the elderly fisherman up the beach making preparations to go to sea in the wee hours of the next morning were his only companions.

Oxy had arrived at the beach in time to see the beginning of the Caribbean sunset, bright red, bright yellow, and the flash of green as the sun slithered below the horizon. Had he chosen another time of day, there would have been some disorder. In the very early morning, in addition to the sights and sounds of the harbor traffic, he would have been distracted by the bustle of folks making their early morning visits to Bayside and the mangrove nearby, and at midday, the crowds of commerce and the midday sun would hinder solemn reflection. Sunset was the perfect time.

From his perfectly positioned perch, Oxy had a panoramic view of the eclectic scenery. He could see the striking colors of the changing horizon to his left, and the gray concrete monstrosity of the Indian merchant a little farther to his left. Although the fishermen's wharf and the public market were some distance away to his right, he could still see the grunge of the back wall, and the fish and meat market beyond. He could see smoke from the city dump and from nearby coal kilns behind him. The center of the harbor was directly ahead, reflecting the twinkling lights of the businesses at the water's edge on the far side. It was his favorite setting for ruminating. Sitting close to the fine white sand and clear, flat blue water in the tranquility of the late afternoon, Oxy was thankful for the time at his spot, since the completed deep water harbor would ruin it. He gave thanks with soft words, and was grateful that although the deep water harbor would antiquate the stevedore jobs, he had a new one that he was happy with. He silently thanked Beady for that, and for the negotiated deal that guaranteed his freedom.

Oxy thought about Tricia, and the possibilities for their relationship. He believed that their blossoming romance was consequential, and she had been loyal during his troubles with the court. Still, Oxy believed that their relationship would fracture if he did not bring some substance and consistency into his life. As he sat there, a wayward thought took root in Oxy's mind – the kind of thought that had not visited his consciousness since his youthful days with Rachel, and he resolved that he would develop the idea.

He would talk to Tricia as soon as he was able, but before he could finish the thought, his countenance changed; he frowned as he realized that in order to proceed with any plan involving Tricia, he would need the blessing of her aunt. Alice Allen – called Two-Pence-Ha'penny woman when she was out of earshot – was a churchgoing lady with a sometimes toxic personality.

Sister Allen, the name she was referred to by friends, had a bad attitude that had become a permanent part of her personality when, as a juvenile, she began to understand that her younger sister Eva could easily play upon the emotions of their parents, was always going to attract the boys, and would have an easier time navigating her way through life. Watching her younger sister sashay through life engendered bitterness, anger, irritability, and resentment in young Alice Allen. And when her parents bypassed her and sent Eva overseas, the transformation was complete. Alice became a sourpuss.

Alice had planned on being the one assisted and given the blessing of her parents to pursue educational and economic opportunities overseas. She was older, and she believed that, Eva's sunny personality notwithstanding, they were equal in aptitude, quickness, intelligence, and the undertaking of their duties. Her parents never gave her a reason why, but Alice believed it was atonement for their treatment of Eva over her relationship with Lou. She did not direct resentment toward her younger sister, but she did feel a great deal of bitterness toward her parents and she'd never forgiven them. Alice Allen's enchanting niece was the only person able to elicit love from her, and Oxy would have to win her over if his plan was going to work.

Oxy left Bayside, but continued to develop his thought. He was walking along a path next to a paved gutter, built for water management from the hills to the south. He was close to the end of the path and the beginning of paved roads when he was pulled from his contemplation.

"George, wha' you ah do down Bayside this time of day?" Headmaster Looby asked as Oxy exited the path to head home via Baker Street.

The headmaster's informal speech was unusual; he did not often use the colloquial speech of day-to-day conversation in Celadon, but had been using it in deference to the old gentleman he had just finished chatting with. Oxy smiled; he always did when the headmaster called him, because he thought the headmaster's use of his real name was ironic, considering that he was the one who'd given Oxy his nickname. What happened was that Headmaster Looby thought that George was a contradictory personality, so he used the term "oxymoron" to describe him. Oxy's classmates loved the word and nicknamed him Oxymoron, which was later shortened to Oxy.

"Good evening, Mister Looby. I was down there sorting out some things in my mind," Oxy said, standing across the narrow street from Headmaster Looby, who sat in his black Ford Zephyr.

"What were you trying to sort out, young man?" Headmaster Looby asked as he removed a white handkerchief from the left chest pocket of his shirt and cleaned his glasses.

"Well, sir, I was down there considering the turns that my life has taken recently, and what I need to do to keep myself on the straight and narrow, and avoid those turns, because those are usually bad for me," Oxy said.

"You know, young man, I always felt, since your school days, that you had great potential, though so far you've failed to come up to snuff." Headmaster Looby slipped the polished glasses back onto his ears. He studied Oxy, and the man felt like a little boy under his steady gaze. Headmaster Looby nodded, as though satisfied with what he saw. "It's good that you're thinking about things; maybe you will finally reach the standards you have the ability to reach. And yes, I am familiar with those turns in your life. I was told about your recent troubles. Hopefully that's all in the past?"

"Hopefully," Oxy agreed.

"By the way, how is that wonderful woman who is your aunt doing?"

"She is doing well, sir. You know her; her optimism never ends."

"Ok, George, please tell your aunt that I will see her at the next union meeting," Headmaster Looby said.

"I will do that, sir."

Headmaster Looby started his car and drove along Baker Street in the direction of the school compound. Oxy took off in the opposite direction. He had a good feeling about the felicitous meeting and conversation. The headmaster's words gave credence to his view that he was indeed living below his capabilities.

Oxy created a mental list of the things that he needed to do to kick off his new lifestyle. He would talk to Tricia's aunt, but first he'd need to purge his mind of her Two-Pence-Ha'penny persona, created during a brief period of rebellion during which Alice Allen had lived a reckless life. A time when her body was very popular with young men. The nickname had been bestowed on her after a particularly wanton episode.

Second, he must convince Tricia that the task of remaking himself would be a lasting effort and not an Oxy burst. Third, he must tell his kept-women, which would be all his women, that he would be seeing only one woman. Fourth, he must tell the people that he cared for about his plan. His aunt, Beady, his children, and their mother all needed to know.

Oxy's walk home was quick, and he had figured what he needed to do by the time he got there.

"Aunty, I met Headmaster Looby earlier and he asked 'bout you, and say to tell you that he will see you at the next union meeting."

"That's good; it's always nice to hear from him."

Oxy noted what she was wearing. "You look like you going out."

"Yes, I'm going to a public meeting, they go' talk about the progress on the deep water harbor and troubles at the sugar factory. You should come." Aunty stared at Oxy. He didn't have a ready answer and knew what his aunt was thinking. He hoped that she changed the topic, because if she turned her thoughts to words they would heighten his discomfort.

"But before I go to the meeting, I must pass by Wellesley. I hear one of his boys get a dog bite," Aunty said with a puffed chest and a sigh.

"Dog bite!" Oxy exclaimed.

"Yes. They buy him a pair of them ugly brown hoppers from Bata and he run 'cross John Dee backyard to test them out. That cross brindle dog that John Dee own see the little boy running 'cross the yard and take off after he. Them say, the dog grab the little boy foot and wouldn't let go. Somebody say it was the shoes that attract the dog."

Aunty related the incident with gravity, but Oxy had a difficult time containing his laughter. What Aunty did not know was the brown sneakers in question were referred to derisively as mongooses because their color perfectly matched that of the animal. The absurdity of the attack on the shoes by a dog that believed it was chasing a mongoose was just too much for Oxy not to smirk.

Using all his powers to subdue the laughter that was forcing its way to freedom, he said, "Goodnight, Aunty. I'm going to sleep early."

"Something wrong with you; you sick? Why going to sleep so early?" The look on Aunty's face softened.

"No, I'm not sick." Oxy said between throat-clearing coughs. "I do have something to tell you, but I will tell you later."

Aunty was immediately concerned. "Tell me now," she scolded. "I have time; you too like to put off things."

"Okay, okay," Oxy said, forcing his laugh back. "I am going to talk to Tricia's aunt about her. I'm going to change the way I live. I know you going to roll your eyes, but I have come to believe that my future will be one of pain and anguish for myself and the ones that I care about if do not change."

Oxy felt good about his statement because his aunt did not respond with one of her usual and immediate rebuttals. "Hmmm," was the only sound that came from Aunty's mouth.

She was surprised, and toyed with the idea, briefly, that someone had absconded with her nephew and left the copy standing before her as a replacement.

"Listen, Aunty, I will be asleep when you come back from you meeting, so I will see you in the morning," Oxy said.

"Ok, me gone," Aunty replied.

Oxy went about his going-to-bed routine; he took a bath, brushed his teeth, and picked out his clothes for the next day. He lay in his bed and picked up one of the books that Beady had lent him, *Capitalism and Slavery* by Dr. Eric Williams. There was a pile of hardcovers near his bed, including; *The Wretched of the Earth* by Franz Fanon, and *Beyond the Boundary* and *The Black Jacobins* by C. L. R. James. He had been reading *Capitalism and Slavery* for a month, and resolved to pick up the pace and get all the books back to Beady by the promised return date. He read for about half an hour before sleep overtook him.

CHAPTER TWENTY-THREE

The Conflict

Oxy woke, got dressed, ate some porridge (his favorite breakfast), and prepared to walk up to Alice Allen's place. He was pleased with himself for thinking of her as Alice Allen instead of Two-Pence-Ha'penny, and he headed out wearing stylish clothes – the type of clothes usually reserved for first impressions. He had chosen a nearly new, solid green, short-sleeved Ban-Lon shirt; crisp-pressed fatigue pants; and hard shoes – not his comfortable buffalo sandals or his tennis shoes. He had looked at himself in the mirror before he left and decided with a nod that he was firm and fresh.

Sister Allen worked a 10 pm to 6 am shift, and Oxy gambled that she would be a little tired or even worn out, vulnerable to his charms and easier to convince early in the morning. But on that morning he was very wrong.

"Hey, Oxy, weh you ah go so early, and all dress up like that?" A voice shouted from the steps of Mr. Edward's shop. Mr. Edward's shop was located on Celadon Main Road about ten minutes' walk from Aunty's house, and was a popular stop where workmen bought their lunch on their way to work. It was also close to Alice Allen's home.

"Gummy, what you buying?" Oxy shouted back. "Bread and ham-roll? A big man like you still eating that stupidness? You know that nobody in the world know wha' inside ham-roll, not even the people who make it." Oxy chuckled and shook his head.

Gummy had stopped to pick up his bread and ham-roll and a large tin of orange juice before meeting the truck that would take him and the other members of his road crew to their job site.

"No bother 'bout that, me ask you weh you off to, and you no answer me." Gummy walked toward Oxy with purchase in hand, and both men observed each other with playful suspicion.

"Me ah go 'bout me business – my business," Oxy answered, each word delivered slowly for emphasis.

"Okay, sah." Gummy looked away from Oxy, attempting to place his lunch in his lunch bag while walking. He found the space for his bread and ham-roll and orange juice, closed his bag, and continued his journey as Oxy turned off Celadon Main Road toward Alice Allen's house.

"Catch up with you some time, Oxy."

Oxy focused on his imminent talk with Alice Allen. He was uneasy, not sure whether to walk fast or slow. What he planned to do was a first for him. Not the committing to one woman part – well, that too – but the putting himself in the position of a picayune, a small coin. He was on a magician's errand, like a beggar with newsboy cap in hand, to perform the trick of turning the intractable into the agreeable. Confidence bordering on brashness, allure, and caprice – that was Oxy's character. Traits that were fantastic for an action movie star, but often in conflict with the struggles of his daily life. He was entering new territory and needed to go there with a different personality.

He turned onto Tamarind Road, a very short road, and took a deep breath. The people who lived on Tamarind Road were early risers; they were awakened each morning by the shrill crow of the roosters, which, along with the rest of the domesticated fowl and other animals, roamed freely through the neighborhood, sharing the road with Oxy as he approached Alice Allen's place. Folks were up and going through their morning routines; there were even some bright school uniforms about, children who had long walks to school off to an early start. Oxy was two houses from his destination when he heard Palance's voice.

"Hey, wha' you doing 'round here?"

Oxy turned to see Palance stepping onto the road from an alley. The fool's shout did not bother Oxy, and he ignored it. With long strides past the narrow houses, he quickly reached Alice Allen's residence, leaving Palance behind. But Palance followed Oxy to the neat but unpainted picket fence with commination, yapping questions all the while.

"Aunty, look who a' you gap; hoosh you dog 'pon he!" Palance shouted.

Palance was the son of Alice Allen's older brother HoHay, the Celadon vocalization of Jorge, his real name. Jorge and Alice Allen did not share a mother; he was their father's first child. Jorge was born in Panama when their father, like many others from the island, was working on the Panama Canal as a very young man. His father forsook him and returned home, but Jorge, on reaching manhood, left his mother and the only family he knew and traveled as a seaman on a cargo ship in search of his father. His father rejected him, but Jorge remained in Celadon long enough to produce an offspring – Palance – before returning to Panama.

"Boy, me tell you no come 'round me place. Wha' you doing 'round here this early anyway? I see you digging in a alley last week; you must have some woman inside that alley." Alice Allen was pointed and dismissive until Palance walked away.

"Sister Allen, I would like to talk to you please," Oxy said sweetly.

"Walk through the side gate and come in the backyard," Sister Allen instructed pleasantly. She was still wearing her work uniform.

Oxy had not expected a pleasant reception, and he was euphoric as he unhooked the latch on the gate. Oxy started to open the gate, but then he stopped and inquired cautiously, "What about the dog?"

"The dog gone 'bout he business," Sister Allen replied.

Oxy walked through the gate into the backyard. There was a wooden step leading from the back door to the gravel in the yard, an empty clothesline, a stone-heap, a bench of two-by-four-by-eight lumber with concrete blocks as legs, a wooden washstand with a washtub full of clothes being soaked, and some hot pepper trees, planted near the back of the fence. Oxy turned to be sure he had closed the gate properly, took three steps, and stopped. He was not sure what to do next.

"What do you want, George Stevens?" Sister Allen walked down the wooden steps into her backyard and along a short gravel path to the washtub. She faced the washtub with her back to Oxy, who took a moment to look at Sister Allen's form; she was not as pretty as Tricia's mother, but their bodies were similar and dramatic. Oxy opened the conversation timidly.

"I would like to talk to Tricia," he said, misspeaking badly.

"She is not here; she is at a fellowship meeting with the young women at our church," Sister Allen replied.

"Sorry, that is not what I meant," Oxy said to her back. "I meant to say that I want to talk to you about Tricia." He exhaled a breath of relief when he got it right.

"Go ahead, talk. I can wash and listen." Sister Allen had started on a pink blouse, and the squishing sound of her washing made Oxy step closer to hear her clearly. Oxy talked, and he did so tentatively.

"I love Tricia and I believe that she loves me too. We've had some opportunities to talk to each other, but the conversations were constrained because we knew that you wouldn't approve," Oxy explained, getting his confidence back.

"For someone who only believe that Tricia loves you, you certainly taking liberty with that word," Sister Allen argued, and Oxy sensed that she was committed to saying just enough and no more. But she continued, and he wasn't surprised by what she said. "There is no need to go any further. It is not a good idea, this relationship that you want to start with my niece. First, she is a young girl to you. Second, with all you children and their mothers, that is plenty confusion. Why would my niece take on you, and that mess? My answer to you is no; it would be a bad thing."

Sister Allen had stopped washing her clothes and turned to look at Oxy. They were close enough to see the look in each other's eyes, and what Oxy saw in Sister Allen's eyes was certainty. "And also, I know that you and Tyrone are bosom buddies and that you have a good relationship with Ruth, but don't think because of that connection and my close friendship with Ruth that you can use that to your advantage."

Oxy stiffened, and when he spoke his speech was cold. "Sister Allen, I give you the fact that it's your responsibility to look out for and protect Tricia, but I can't let you bad-talk Beady. He is my best friend, and he is also an honorable man." Oxy was upset enough to risk riling Sister Allen, to scrap his mission altogether in defense of his friend. "And I hear you about me and my history. But, I have to say that I will continue to see your niece if she wants to see me, and it will happen without the assistance or the involvement of friends or relations. Thank you for allowing me to have this conversation with you."

Oxy finished and went on his way without waiting for Sister Allen's response.

CHAPTER TWENTY-FOUR
RayRay Reconsiders

Oxy's close encounter with confinement was a hot topic in Celadon, and none except for little children, who were sent to play when hot topics were discussed, were indifferent to his plight, including Rachel. Oxy's troubles affected Rachel's thoughts, and when her boys began asking for their father, she wondered if they had gone to play when sent.

On this day, Rachel's drive home was unusually quiet. The boys were not being their usual boisterous selves, and as she thought about it, Malcolm spoke up.

"Mommy, I would like to spend more time with daddy." His glum manner troubled Rachel.

"Yes, Mommy, me too," Ali concurred in the same morose tone as his brother. Rachel was taken by surprise. She had planned to have discussions with her boys about their father, just not that day.

"Boys, I will talk to you about it when we get home; we should not talk about it while I am driving."

She drove a Hillman Husky – a two-door vehicle bought with the assistance of Mr. Jacobs, her father, who had owned a similar vehicle when he'd lived in London. Rachel was a member of the small group of women in Celadon who drove a car and of an even smaller group of women who owned one, which added to her acclaim. But more important to her than driving a car was driving one without rear doors, which allowed her keep her eyes on the road without worrying about doors being unlocked accidentally. However, her sons were unlocking a different kind of door with their request and she was glad for a reprieve even as disquiet set in.

"Okay, Mommy." The boys agreed to her request to delay the conversation in identical sullen tones, and Rachel pondered their request the rest of the way home to her parents' house.

The story of Rachel's parents is an uplifting narrative. Her father, Mr. Jacobs, was born in Celadon, finished school at age sixteen, and promptly secured a position at the sugar factory as a lathe trainee. He also learned to play the saxophone, and hoped to play with the island's number one band, which was usually comprised of veteran musicians. But due to the band's popularity and the band leader's avarice, the band would be scheduled to play at two, sometimes three venues simultaneously. This was accomplished with a contingent of inexperienced musicians, brought in to make up numbers and play alongside the veteran members. Mr. Jacobs's dedication to his music and his friendship with the band leader's son provided him the opportunity to audition, and then to be invited to play.

He loved the music, and continued practicing and playing even when he moved to Hackney, East London. There, he attended Hackney Technical School to build on his training at the sugar factory, and used what he learned to propel himself into positions of responsibility with bigger pay packets. His diligence at work, and his desire to leave cold, wet London and return to the mango trees, sugarcane, and bayside of his homeland were incentive enough for him to save half the weekly earnings from his day job, all the earnings from the many engagements of the band he played with in London, and the earnings from his work as a freelance musician.

Mr. Jacobs's drive, his brain, his command of the English language, and his easy-to-love personality allowed him to effortlessly navigate the obstacle course of bigotry in 1950s London. Soon

CreateSpace
7290 Investment Drive Suite B
North Charleston, SC 29418

Question About Your Order?
Log in to your account at www.createspace.com and "Contact Support."

12/10/2015 07:35:46 PM
Order ID: 104850905

Qty.	Item

IN THIS SHIPMENT

5	At The Rainbow's Very End
	0692324135

PS_BX0514841

he was a supervisor at his workplace, and he used his position to learn the fine points of running a business and a lathe shop. Mr. Jacobs's woman, Mabel, his love since she was a tasteful teenager, joined him in England, where they were married. She embarked on training to become nurse, and they continued their quest to return home. Rachel was born two years after Mabel's arrival in London; and fourteen years after stepping onto a launch at the city jetty on the first leg of his journey to England, Mr. Jacobs flew back to his homeland with his wife and daughter.

Mr. Jacobs's return home was preceded by a shipment of tools and accessories from his lathe shop. He had acquired the shop from an Englishman who was destroyed financially by his fondness for a game of chance that was readily available at the racetracks and betting houses that dotted the city of London.

On his return to Celadon, Mr. Jacobs started a business and built a house on land he had purchased while still living in London. The house was built on a hill, and the view from the backyard featured a green valley with a dry ravine and rolling hills. The property was located at the boundary of Celadon, where the cane and cotton fields began, and the house was erected in a fruit orchard of avocado, guava, papaya, mango, custard apple, pomegranate, and coconut trees, which Mr. Jacobs's representatives in Celadon had planted while he'd charted his return from Hackney. It was a comfortable home for Rachel and her sons.

As she pulled up to the house, Rachel's mind was full of consideration for her sons and their father; she wished the unpleasant conversation could be postponed. The boys loved to be with their father, and the easy personality that had enchanted her also worked on their sons. She dared to consider that lately Oxy had been showing signs of maturity. Rachel parked in the driveway at the side of the house and exited the car.

"Boys, you be certain that you remove everything from the car that should be removed from the car. I know you must be tired, but I would appreciate it." The boys did what they were asked to do quietly, and walked past their mom, who waited near the front of the car.

It had been a silent ride home after their brief conversation, and Rachel was grateful for it. It had been some time since she'd had to consider the dynamics of Oxy's relationship with his sons. Life itself was a difficult assignment, and being a single mother raising twin boys made it more so. Keeping up with active boys and having a full-time job did not leave a lot of time for that kind of introspection.

Rachel walked up the steps behind Malcolm and Ali, through a side door into the kitchen, where the boys placed the items they had brought into the house onto counters and into cupboards.

"Goodnight, Grandma! Goodnight, Grandpa!" The boys shouted brightly. They were animated now, and ran from the kitchen into the front of the house.

Rachel smiled and followed them to the dining room, pleased that her sons had recovered their energy.

"Good evening, Mother and Father." Rachel greeted, and hugged her mother, who had risen from the dining table.

"I know you went to a school fête, but I have to ask: you'll want something to eat?" Mabel, who was still an elegant woman, looked at her daughter admiringly.

"No," Rachel responded. "They are full. They tried to eat everything that was edible at the fête, especially dandy balls, and they are tired. Just time for them to clean themselves up and go to bed."

"Ok," her mother agreed, and walked into the kitchen

"Father, how was your day?"

"My day was a good one, my child."

Rachel was leaning against the frame of the entrance to the dining room, but moved to the dining table when her mother returned with a pot of bush tea and poured a cup for her husband and one for her daughter. Rachel sipped her tea, and the boys went to get ready for bed.

"You know, I could give them some sour-sop bush tea. That would certainly put them to bed quick and make them rest well tonight," Mabel suggested playfully. Her chuckle infected her daughter and husband, and they all had a good laugh.

"Mother, Father, Malcolm and Ali told me that they want to spend more time with their father."

Rachel's announcement transformed Mr. Jacobs's features, and his body went rigid. The change in his bearing was contagious and there was a dramatic change of atmosphere as Rachel's statement tugged at everyone's emotions.

"What did you tell them, Rachel?" It was Mabel who spoke first, shaking her head from side to side.

"I told them that we would talk about it later; I was driving at the time. I will talk to them before they go to sleep."

Rachel looked intently at her parents, acknowledging without words that they were the source of her strength. It was her father who spoke next.

"George is a man now, and he will be judged by what he shows in the face of difficulties and his willingness to take on his responsibilities; it is when a man faces discomfort and inconvenience that he should demonstrate whether he will bend or stand up straight."

Mr. Jacobs was a prudent man; prudent with words, judicious with his decisions. He had given considerable thought to Oxy's relationship with his daughter and his grandsons and was neutral on the matter – the opposite of his wife, who was not fond of Oxy. But Mr. Jacobs had seen promise in Oxy when he was a teenager, and felt that perhaps with the correct motivation, he could live up to that early potential.

Mabel, a woman of high standards, could not so easily give Oxy a break. "I know that our burdens are not heavy, but the calamity that is George's life would crush us."

Mabel's disfavor would not allow her to consider a reclamation project. Her idea of a good man was her husband; she did not believe that he was the *only* good man, but she did believe that he was the *measure* of a good man – and George did not measure up.

Rachel heard running footsteps and raised herself from her seat. "Mother, Father, I hear both of you, but I need to think about this." Rachel increased the volume of her voice so that her sons would hear. "Wait just a minute, boys!"

She caught up with the twins in the hallway. Then she put her left arm on Malcolm's shoulder, her right arm on Ali's shoulder, and led them to their bedroom.

"Boys, I understand that you want to spend more time with your father. I will get in touch with him and talk to him about it. Now say your prayers and go to bed."

"Yes, Mommy," the boys answered in unison.

The boys settled into their beds, and Rachel adjusted the sheets and secured the bedroom window before sitting down at the foot of the bed farthest from the door.

"Boys, it looks like we need to get you bigger beds; you are outgrowing these."

Sleep was overtaking Malcolm and Ali fast, and their subdued responses made Rachel smile. She stood and moved between the two beds, where she leaned over, opened her right palm, placed it against Malcom's cheek, and performed her nightly ritual:

"Night is nigh,
Daylight gone,
The sun is no longer in the sky,
Rest my child,
God gave me a treasure the day you were born."

Then she turned toward the other bed, placed her palm against Ali's cheek, and repeated the lullaby. The ritual was always soothing to the boys and to her, too. This was the best part of her day. She walked from the room slowly, like she did every night, and left the bedroom door ajar.

Rachel sighed as she opened the door to her own room, but when she was inside she decided to forego her evening chores. Instead, she showered and changed, planning to go sit in the courtyard.

The urbane Mr. Jacobs had built a courtyard with a gazebo, and that was where Rachel intended to go and contemplate Oxy. As she prepared to go outside, she examined her options, and they were few. It had been a long time since she'd even considered George; she had put him away, and took him out only when his visits with his sons made that necessary. As she pondered, there was a knock at her door, followed by an inquiry.

"Will you be going to bed now?" Mabel asked.

"No, Mother, I will be going out back to sit and think," Rachel replied. Mabel heard the weariness in her daughter's voice and worried for her.

"I understand. Things will work out; they usually do." Mabel paused. "Your father and I will be going to bed now. Goodnight, my child, and see you in the morning."

"Goodnight, Mother," Rachel replied, then began to search through the contents of her dressing table. It was a quick search that ended when she determined that she had left the item in her bathroom, and stopped there to retrieve it on her way out into the evening air.

Mr. Jacobs was Celadon to his bones; nevertheless, he had grown accustomed to some of the niceties of the English lifestyle, which he had gladly brought home to his beloved island. The gazebo and courtyard at the back of the Jacobs's property were among those niceties. It was newly dark when Rachel sat down in the gazebo, but if it had been daytime, butterflies, honey bees, and hummingbirds would have been seen at work in the nearby garden, pecking for the sweet nectar of hibiscus and honeysuckle flowers. The mosquitoes had fed earlier and were not a nuisance. The air was fragrant, so she took a deep breath and looked up at the sky. The glare from the lamppost at the front of the house was the only light competing with the stars. It was a starry night, and it was easy to find the Big Dipper. There was no moon.

Rachel began her self-examination by evaluating her relationship with Oxy. The current state of their relationship was clear to her: Oxy entered her mind only when she had to make arrangements for their sons to meet with him. So she started at the beginning, listed all the things that had caused injury to their relationship, and then moved on to the prognosis for healing it. It was a solemn and deliberate undertaking, but one that she understood was necessary. She thought about the person she had been at the start of their relationship, a girl who bore no resemblance to the woman she had become, a woman who often referred to their past association, when friends asked, as the inexperience of youth.

Rachel looked out into the night, a darkness that was interrupted by the occasional firefly, then breathed an involuntary sigh. She realized that she was using the thumb and index finger of her left hand to play with the pendant on the chain around her neck – the chain she had misplaced earlier, prompting the hurried search on her way out. The realization gave Rachel a jolt, for the chain was a relic from the past. Yet it had remained around her neck through her transition into adulthood, and during her years of study in England. She wondered why she had kept it. The reason, when it came, directed her to a new avenue of possibilities.

The next morning, Rachel was the last to sit down to the varied fare that was breakfast. Mabel was having fish left over from the prior night's dinner, while Mr. Jacobs was satisfying his taste for English breakfast with fried eggs, sausages, and baked beans with toast. Rachel and the boys had oatmeal.

"Good morning, Mother. Good morning, Father. Good morning, Malcolm and Ali. Did you have a good night's rest?" Rachel asked her parents, in her still-not-entirely-alert morning voice.

"Yes, and woke up early enough to prepare this breakfast," Mabel replied with a hint of pride in her voice.

"Boys, did you thank your grandmother for preparing this breakfast?" Rachel looked across the table at Malcolm and Ali with raised eyebrows.

"Thank you for breakfast, Grandma," the boys chorused.

"Mother, Father, I have an announcement. I will have a talk with George to see how we can arrange to have the boys spend more time with him."

"Thank you, Mommy!" the boys exclaimed.

"I don't know how you plan to do it, but best of luck to you." Mr. Jacobs's reply was cool and noncommittal, while his wife's response was a barely perceptible groan.

CHAPTER TWENTY-FIVE
The Union

After the favor on behalf of Oxy, Beady's slight doubt was gone; the union job was working out. An important union person had delivered, kept his friend out of jail, and that reinforced Beady's commitment to the cause. He immersed himself in his training, in learning labor union business, and soon began to put his new skills to use.

Pinto's workers had been holding meetings after work at Margie's food shop to eat, drink, and bond as they discussed making their workplace a union shop. Beady had provided them with the union literature, and they had elected to sign up.

"The first thing that we need to do is to get the union in the shop all proper and legal," Beady said to the workers who had gathered at Margie's on a Friday afternoon.

"Margie, the food ready?" a short, thick, mature gentleman interrupted. He wore a brown felt hat and was dressed in work clothes. He was called Walrus because of his fleshy cheeks, thick lips, and extended canines.

"Everything almost ready, me just taking off the fig leaf (banana tree leaf)."

"Well hurry up, I have been dreaming of putting knife and fork to your ducana," the jovial Walrus instructed, and Margie laughed.

On the wharf near the public market, Margie's was comprised of a wooden shed, wooden tables, wooden benches, and a concrete floor. The meal of the day was Margie's renowned ducana and saltfish. Her legend included the story of the time she had prepared a batch of her ducana for some friends to take on a private, Friday night, moonlit picnic. At the end of their outing, Margie's friends forgot a few of the sweet potato dumplings in the trunk of their car and did not remember to remove them until Monday morning. When they did remember the ducana and open the wrapping, the dumplings were as soft and as fresh as they were when Margie took them from the pot.

"Okay, Walrus, hush up; the food will get here when it ready," Beady scolded. The man fell silent at once, and Beady continued. "Compatriots, we are almost there. All that is required is for the company to sign off and the union will be in there to safeguard your health and prosperity."

"Beady, you sure they go' sign off?" Walrus asked, concerned.

"Don't worry about that; that is only a formality. The company has no choice; it is the law of the land." Beady was emphatic, putting to use his union lessons on effective communication. "Anybody have any questions?"

Beady was sitting on a stool, his back against the counter. Margie was behind him, moving here and there, hands busy and sweat rolling down her dark, smooth, cherubic face. The union prospects sat at the tables; and Beady, per his training, tried to look everyone in the eye as he asked for questions, searching for flickers of uncertainty and to ascertain whether he had turned on the light.

"Beady, are you sure that we not getting any trouble from the Pintos?" The question was asked by a twentyish young man, the youngest worker. His name was Worrell and he wore a gray collarless jacket and pants – the style made popular by the Beatles – and had plans that evening to go to the Town House, a popular venue for touring American soul singers.

"No, in this country we have laws that protect the rights of workers; you have the absolute right to join a union."

The questioner heard the finality of Beady's response and was satisfied.

"Now, I need to take an official vote and record it. Not having Miss John, Mrs. Williams, and Marilyn here does not bar us from having a vote today." Beady turned, stretching to pick up a clipboard and pen from the counter, and adjusted his light-blue "bossa nova" shirt – short, without tails and a waistband – to cover the gap that had appeared between it and the waistband of his gray slacks. It had been a short journey from the first discussions and contact with Beady to the vote.

All the workers at Pinto's were ready, and there was no need for further persuasion. The union was the most powerful entity on the island. Political parties were a thought but not a reality; the union leaders and their associates were also the elected representatives to the Legislative Council and appointees to the Executive Council or Cabinet. In the eyes of the citizenry, the union had fought a heroic fight, fired up the working class, defeated the old plantation class, and changed the politics and economics of the island. The union held sway over what did and did not occur on the island, and the workers from Pinto's knew it.

With all that she had to contend with behind the counter, Margie had kept her ears on the proceedings and expertly informed the gathering, in her angelic voice, that "Food ready," at the moment she picked up that voting was completed – in favor of joining the union.

"That voice always amaze me, it so sweet and beautiful." Beady was standing now, talking to Margie across the counter, while the workers had assumed the ready to eat position.

No one volunteered to help Margie serve or to serve themselves; they all just sat expectantly until Margie shouted at them. Beady led the way and began filling a plate with the food that Margie had placed on the counter. Everyone present was pleased with themselves and their prospects going forward.

After securing the votes and attempting to get the Pintos' assent, Beady reported to union headquarters to give his boss an update.

"I am genuinely surprised that we are having trouble with the Pintos," the general secretary of the union said, although he really wasn't surprised because he believed that at every opportunity the powerful attempted to keep the underclass in their place.

"I am not saying that the Pintos are representative of the past, but you must always remember that since man started writing things down, there has always been gradation of mankind into an austere and blunt social classification – a small gang controlled all the natural resources, government, church, the courts, the military, and business. This gang, referring to themselves as elites or the gilded, profited from hereditary wealth, power, and privilege, while the rest were condemned to lives of poverty, indignity, and extreme compliance," the general secretary soapboxed. "Few people questioned the social order; it was considered divine. Folks worked, lived, and died within their station. Interclass mobility was extremely rare, and challenging. The labor movement, with its warts, was one of the most successful attempts in history to awaken the hoi polloi, and bring them to general betterment. The Honorable and associates founded the union in that tradition, and inculcated the people with knowledge and confidence."

Beady, although new to the job, had quickly grown into his role and spoke to his boss with confidence. "It's a surprise all around, because their say-so is just a formality, just a courtesy we pay them, to let them know what is going on." He paused. "I am getting good reactions from the workers. We have some disciple types, some dissidents, and some agitators. I never expected that type of diversity from such a small group, but everyone is in, no mixed feelings."

"Mrs. Pinto believes that she can count on her relationship with the Honorable to get some kind of special dispensation," the general secretary revealed.

"So that is what's behind their obstinacy?" Beady asked.

"Yes, but she must understand that with this, you friends can't help you." The general secretary took a deep breath. "Yes, Tyrone, that is the nature of the likes of Mrs. Pinto. You need to call a strike." He rapped loudly on his desk, startling Beady and conveying his passion for the task he had assigned.

The Pintos were of a group of merchants – well-off merchants – who were not the beneficiaries of hereditary position and wealth like most of the privileged people on island. They were of Portuguese lineage, from a group of migrants who had advanced themselves through hard work, business acumen, and the advantage of race. The Honorable and Mrs. Pinto had a long-standing and mutually beneficial friendship. It is said that politics is a bargain between beggars; the Honorable believed this, and he gladly welcomed the Pintos as allies and accepted their resources in the fight against his adversaries in exchange for favors that he was able to provide to them.

"Will the Honorable step in on her behalf?" Beady asked, concerned.

"No, he won't. This is much more than his relationship with the Pintos." The general secretary's answer was quick and assured.

Beady, relieved, replied, "They will be called out on strike next week."

CHAPTER TWENTY-SIX
Joy and Heartbreak

Oxy was a bit disheartened after his chat with Alice Allen, but happiness sometimes comes without being called, and he was about to have a visit that would transform his life.

Rachel, never one to "um" and "ah," sent a message to Oxy, and made plans to have him come to the house for a Sunday afternoon dinner. Oxy was surprised but pleased by the invitation. He had not permitted himself the luxury of thinking about Rachel in some time, but with the invitation, all of his dormant feelings about her flooded his heart. The boys were his delight, and every visit with them was a wonderful adventure, but Rachel bewildered him.

The message he received from Rachel's mother, as relayed to him by Mabel's helper, instructed him to come to the house around midday on Sunday. A dinner with the whole family? He had a fair relationship with Rachel's father, but his relationship with her mother was tricky. However, he felt that on balance, being in the presence of the exquisite Rachel was worth it, even with her habitual frostiness. Besides, spending extended time with his sons would certainly offset his misgivings about Rachel's mother.

On the day of the dinner, Rachel stood in the kitchen with Mabel, preparing the meal and talking.

"Mother, I know that this plan of mine makes you uncomfortable, but this is the best way to start a conversation with George; I promised the boys, and they have been asking already." Rachel smiled at the thought of the boys, and her mother smiled too. "Malcolm and Ali are keen to see their father, and keep asking when, when, when at every opportunity."

Oxy arrived shortly before midday. It was not a hot day, but one of gentle breezes and soft sunshine. He was dressed neatly but without his usual flash. The fifteen-minute walk to the Jacobs home was comfortable, so there was no perspiration when he got there. Malcolm and Ali had been playing sentinels, keeping watch since their return from church. They saw their father approaching and came running down the front steps and across the stone walkway; they were at the gate by the time Oxy reached it and helped him with the latch. As soon as he was through, they grabbed him and swung onto an arm apiece.

"Daddy, Daddy, we are so glad that you are here! You don't know how glad we are." Malcolm had detached himself from his father's arm and was jumping and skipping around him as Oxy hoisted Ali onto his shoulder.

Rachel appeared at the front door, wearing a perfectly fitting, sleeveless aqua dress with a white Peter Pan collar and buttons from neck to waist, designed to give the impression of skirt and blouse.

"Good morning, Rachel. How was church today?" Oxy greeted, lowering his son from his shoulder as he walked toward Rachel, who was moving toward him across the porch.

"Church was good. How are you doing today?" Rachel reached the front steps. She ran her open palm over Ali's head as his father put him down at her feet.

"I am doing well, and I am glad to be here." Oxy felt a little lighter when he detected not warmth, but at least a not-so-frosty Rachel. "The boys are full of energy today; it is always a challenge to keep pace with them." Oxy looked at his sons with admiration.

"Let us go inside." Rachel turned and walked back across the porch, then opened and went through the front door, calling, "Father, Mother, George is here," as she rejoined her mother in the kitchen.

Oxy offered his greetings to Mabel, then went to join Mr. Jacobs, who was sitting in a Morris chair listening, via a short-wave radio, to the BBC World Service. The older man raised his index finger and indicated a chair across from his. Oxy took the signal to remain silent, and contented himself with sitting quietly and listening to the end of the news broadcast. Afterwards, Mr. Jacobs invited Oxy to walk to the gazebo for a chat.

"It is a wonderful day," Mr. Jacobs said, when both men had settled under the gazebo. "I hope we have a few more days like this for the rest of the week. We are due some good days, so I hope the rain holds off. We could always use it on this island, but I fall out with rain a long time ago." He chuckled at the memory of the drizzly days that were the norm in England. He was in a mellow mood as he sat on a marble bench, looking beyond at the valley and rolling hills that were created as if for artists to paint. For Oxy, the day was pleasant for other reasons, and he spoke about it.

"I have not been to your house in a long time; I am hoping this invitation is a favorable sign. Even if it rains, it will be a very wonderful day."

"George, all I can tell you is that this visit can potentially bring you closer to your sons."

Before Oxy could respond, he heard familiar sounds behind him and stood up to see the boys running toward them from the house.

"Daddy, can we go walkabout?" they said together, as they often did.

"Boys, let me go talk to your mother about that. I will be back in a minute. Talk to your grandfather."

Oxy touched Ali on his head before walking back to the kitchen, where Rachel and her mother were still preparing dinner.

He told her about the boys' request, and Rachel agreed without her usual questions or lectures. She only asked that the walkabout not last longer than twenty minutes; dinner would be ready by then. Oxy returned to the boys quickly, and happily told them the plan for the walkabout.

"Boys, let's head west; there are some cherry trees down that way. When I was a schoolboy, our Friday afternoon recess lasted all afternoon, beginning just after lunch until the end of the school day, and we would sometimes spend the afternoon exploring Cherry Harbor. And—"

Father and sons were on their way, and the boys cut him off halfway through his recollection, but that did not matter because the joy of watching Malcolm and Ali perform short sprints and jump around mimicking the antics of young goats was enough.

"It's a good thing I brought this plastic bag – ta-da!" Oxy said as he pulled the bag from his pocket.

"Daddy, you knew that we were going to come here; that's why you brought the plastic bag with you," Malcolm said, giggling.

"Son, I only got it from the kitchen when I went to talk to your mother. That's when I got the idea. Remember, boys, we can't eat too many of the cherries; we going to have dinner shortly. We can put most of what we pick in the plastic bag."

When they reached their destination, the boys giggled and pranced, dinner far from their minds. They filled half the bag with two of every three cherries they picked from spiky branches, and then the little gang searched nearby for additional fruit-bearing trees. They found some guavas and golden apples, and after plucking them from their branches, they stopped and looked down onto a scenic dale. The scene encompassed a cane field, a meandering creek, and an old sugar mill located at the end of the locomotive line. Oxy took the opportunity to give the boys a geography lesson, explaining the source of the creek, pointing out its delta, and identifying landmarks in the distance for his curious boys. He was overwhelmed by the emotions of a proud father and teacher by the time he herded them back to the house.

"What you all bring back today?" Mr. Jacobs asked the boys as they ran to him, their father trailing. He was still sitting just where they'd left him, under the gazebo.

"Grandpa, Grandpa, we get some cherry and some guava and a golden apple, and we try to find some macaw, and try to get some cashew meat, but they were not ripe yet."

Malcolm joined his brother, who had gotten there first, next to their grandfather and passed the bag to him for review. Mr. Jacobs looked at their stash with genuine approval.

"Hmmm," Mr. Jacobs said. "A good haul; this should last you and Ali a while. Now, I hope you boys didn't eat too much of them guava, because too much guava make you hard-bound."

Oxy confirmed Mr. Jacobs's assessment. "You don't have to worry about them and constipation from too much guava; their father has had that experience and they were told. Let me take these inside."

He took the bag of fruits from Mr. Jacobs and walked to the kitchen with the boys, where their grandmother took the plastic bag, and their mother offered a light reprimand about their appearance.

"Boys, you know that you need to clean up before we eat," Rachel instructed.

When the boys had left to clean themselves, Rachel called softly, "George."

And Oxy replied softly, emboldened by her invitation to dinner and her manner throughout the day. "Yes, RayRay?"

"George, I invited you here because I want you to talk to you about spending a lot more time with your sons," she explained. "That means spending more time with me, and maybe a way back into my life."

There was a smile on her lips as she said this. Her eyes searched his, her head cocked. It was the kind of look he hadn't seen for many years, and it made him want things again.

"I have been a wandering rogue; it seems that now I am being beckoned home." Oxy's words were meant to be a statement but sounded like a question when they flowed from his mouth.

"Yes, you are," Rachel answered.

Mabel did not speak, but she directed a disapproving look and a groan at Rachel and Oxy from her position in front of the stove. Rachel broke Oxy's gaze to address her disgruntled mother.

"Mother, I know that you heard what I said to George, and I chose this moment to say it to him because I wanted you to hear me say it. Mother, it's the way it will be." Rachel didn't speak harshly, but she was firm. She crossed the kitchen and gently touched Mabel's cheek, a fond look on her face.

A flummoxed Oxy stared at them but didn't move. Of all the ways he'd imagined the day would turn out, this was not one of them. He was enjoying his good fortune, looking intently at mother and daughter, when Rachel left her mother's side, walked up to him, leaned in, and kissed him lightly on the lips.

"I guess that was the punctuation mark," Mabel joked, coming to terms, quickly, with her daughter's decision, then announced, "We are ready to eat."

Oxy worked hard to contain his excitement, but it was a difficult job. He might have had his fingers crossed behind his back. He did not want to let go of a moment that offered the prospect of a new life featuring Rachel and his sons. He held on until he was the last to sit at the dinner table.

After the meal of rice with pigeon peas, stewed beef, carrots and potatoes, string beans, and steamed cabbage, Rachel and Oxy left the boys with their grandparents and walked to the gazebo. They sat and sipped ginger beer made by her father (it was his favorite drink).

Rachel offered Oxy uninvited visiting rights, within reason; access to his sons in keeping with the current living arrangements, his and theirs; and the opportunity to be with them on more of their outings. Oxy was grateful for what was offered, but her silence on the matter of her expectations was disquieting. Did she expect him to know what was required of him? Oxy feared that the penalty for failing to measure up could be very high. He thought briefly about the things that he would be willing to give up for this new life, but there were too many considerations to go through at that moment.

Instead, he prepared to enjoy the company of his sons, for Malcolm and Ali had left the house, and were clamoring toward their parents. Rachel smiled at them on her way back to the house. The boys proved to be an ample distraction, keeping Oxy busy kicking and throwing balls and running around. Nevertheless, he had moments to contemplate the weight of his quandary. A decision was inescapable, and while wicket-keeping a cricket game with his sons, Oxy resolved that he needed to have grim talks with Tricia, Beady, and his aunt. Both he and the boys had worn themselves out by the time Oxy bid farewell to his sons and the Jacobs's in the late afternoon.

He headed to Bayside when he left; there was still enough light left for him to visit his spot on the beach. He tried to figure the origin of his good fortune – what deed, what prior act he had committed. He sat on his stump for a short time, because it didn't take long for him to make a decision in the late afternoon.

The evening light was fading when he left the beach; a crisp orange sun halfway below the horizon, moving quickly out of sight. Oxy strolled home along a familiar path. Although his mind was made up, there was a longing for the elation he had felt the last time he sat on his stump. Then, it was all positive – there had been no need to break hearts or disappoint anyone. As he walked, he responded with only a brief hello or nod to the folks who greeted or approached him, and was able to make it to his place in half the normal time.

Oxy did not sleep well that night. He kept himself awake rehearsing the three chats that he planned to have – with Aunty, with Beady, and with Tricia.

As he envisioned the one with Tricia, it would take five minutes – a short chat, better to ease the pain and discomfort for both of them. Oxy was mistaken. When Tricia was able to share five minutes with him, the break room felt like the bottom of the bay: no air, a crushing force, and the inability to produce words. He sat for a few seconds looking at her, working his way out of constriction until he found the words.

"Tricia, I need to talk to you about something … but not now," he fumbled.

Oxy understood that delay would complicate matters, but emotional swings, from joy to regret to joy, were overwhelming him.

"That's okay, we can talk about it later," Tricia said. The break room was empty except for them, two sad souls devoid of cheer, full of gloom.

"George, I have some not so good news," Tricia said. Oxy stiffened but waited for her to continue. "I moved in with Beady and Ruth yesterday. But it is a temporary arrangement." Tricia forced a smile, but her delivery was unusually dull.

"What!" Oxy exclaimed. "What do you mean, you moved in temporarily with Beady and Ruth? What happened between you and your aunt?" His surprise and angst caused him to raise his voice.

"Sorry," he offered, but still she remained silent, so he pressed. "Talk to me, Tricia."

"Okay, we have been having difficulties recently. I told her that as an adult I need to take control of my life and make my own decisions, and that has been the cause of friction between us. Yesterday after church, all fall down. So, Sister Ruth suggested that we separate for a bit, and work things out from afar."

Tricia sighed, and Oxy felt the wind going out of him too; things had just gotten more complicated.

They parted company, both feeling low and on emotional reserve. Oxy had given himself a reprieve, but later in the day when he told Tricia about Rachel's offer, and what the offer meant, he poured gloom on top of misery. Tricia was distraught and would remain that way for some time.

CHAPTER TWENTY-SEVEN

The Riot

Monday morning, the first day of the strike, was like most days on the island. The sky was clear and blue. The sun appeared at six-thirty, and it was already a warm day when the picket line was set up. Pinto's management team arrived at seven and was unsettled by the activities in front of their business. The managers shuffled by their employees, both groups giving each other questioning looks but not saying a word.

"Walrus, you see the look on them face?" Worrell asked. The youngster was the most animated worker on the picket line, in stark contrast to the composed figure of Beady who patrolled the line.

"What you think them go' do today?" Walrus asked, his lips curled, thick moustache concealing his smile.

"Me think them go' try an' run th' place by them self." Worrell nodded slowly.

"Well, make them try." Walrus spiked every word with defiance.

Pinto's was located on one of the busiest streets in the city. Whether going to work or just going about their daily business, pedestrians from Celadon and from the south and southeast of the city walked by Pinto's, which was also near the public market. Most passersby that morning were supportive of the picketers and their greetings encouraged Walrus, Worrell, and their coworkers.

"Hold the line, hold the line."

Every new face that walked by repeated the mantra. When the sun got hotter, the picketers took turns in the shade of a nearby tree, but lost none of the enthusiasm that they had begun the day with. As the day progressed, traffic in and out of the business decreased, and the picketers observed that fact with delight, and some mild taunts for the few who'd ventured inside. Still, there were no significant incidents, and the picketers held the line chanting until the end of the workday.

Beady was the boss of the picket line and had information suggesting that the Pintos were considering bringing in scabs. He did not believe it, but he was aware that there were enough rascals and scoundrels about to not take chances. Therefore, he asked the workers to show up half an hour early for the next day's activities.

On the second day of the picket line, Beady arrived early in the union van.

"Good morning, you all sleep alright? You ready?" he asked Headley and Weekes, who comprised one of the two-man teams that drove the delivery trucks at Pinto's.

"Good morning, Beady. You believe that today will be incident-free like yesterday?" Headley asked.

Headley had won the race against Weekes to the little red van, but Weekes was not far behind, and together they unloaded the picket signs.

"I think so. I don't believe we will have any trouble today," Beady replied.

Weekes and Headley were named for West Indies cricketers Everton Weekes and George Headley. Headley was the first black man to captain a West Indies cricket team and Weekes was a cricketing legend and ferocious batsman whose first name had been popular for boys born when he was at the height of his game. Celadon's Headley was the father of three and a lay preacher. Weekes was a decade younger, childless, and spent his weekends crashing parties and sinking boats (the act of devouring all the food available and depleting the host's stock of liquor).

By the time Weekes and Headley had unloaded and were ready to distribute the signs, all the picketers had arrived. Present were the cashiers – Janice, a single mother in her mid-twenties, and the matronly Mrs. Williams, senior cashier in the grocery. Also present were the stock men, Worrell and Fidel, both just entering adulthood. Worrell was named for another cricketer, Frank Worrell, a teammate of Everton Weekes. Fidel had gotten his nickname because of his fiery rhetoric and revolutionary zeal.

Patrick and Winston, the other pickup truck team, had arrived eating their breakfast, and were standing next to the eatery team, which included Walrus, the cook; Miss Pearl, the server; and Marilyn, the eatery cashier. Miss Pearl and Marilyn had arrived with Mary, the office assistant, and everyone wore clothes that highlighted the union colors.

Pinto's, with its red neon sign, was unique on the island – a convincing attempt to bring an American business innovation to the Caribbean. It was the island's only combination eatery, grocery, and hard goods store. Other businessmen had opened stand-alone cafés with soda fountains where beverages, ice cream shakes, American-style hamburgers, and hot dogs were sold, but none matched Pinto's combination operation.

At eight o'clock, the scabs arrived. They were a scruffy-looking bunch; they had to be, because they were rascals and scoundrels. Now, imagine a cheerful Caribbean morning: blue sky, colorful shirts, colorful blouses, colorful pants, and colorful skirts, birds flying about, children wearing brightly colored uniforms on their way to school, smiling faces, and white teeth. Now imagine large rain clouds, turning the blue sky to gray, making all the bright colors dull, and turning all the smiles into frowns. The scabs were the rain clouds.

They were about to enter Pinto's when the sound of shattered glass disrupted the orderly morning. Someone had thrown a stone at the scabs, and it had hit a window.

"Oh, shit!" Walrus said.

"Who the hell do that?" Beady asked, standing on tiptoe and stretching his neck, attempting to get a better look at the entrance of the business.

"I believe that it is somebody from the gallery," Fidel offered, referring to the group of onlookers who'd showed up to support the picketers. The gallery was a mix of men, women, and youngsters, the latter showing up before and after school.

The picketers walked quietly to and fro using the public sidewalk across from their workplace. The onlookers in the gallery, although on the sidewalk, were further away, and were vocal and antsy. They had arrived expecting drama and they wanted confrontation. The striking workers had not planned for strike breakers, and were expecting neither scabs nor trouble. Yet, there it was.

The mood had changed, and the striking workers were preparing to move into position closer to the Pinto's building and away from the gallery. Beady felt he had to reduce the tension, so he stood in the street facing the picketers and began calling their names.

"Walrus, Fidel, Weekes, Headley, Patrick and Winston, Worrell, Miss Pearl, Marilyn, Mrs. Williams, Mary, Janice." Beady called every one, looking at each person directly as he said their name. He wanted to have everyone's attention before he spoke. Patrick and Winston, the shortest and the tallest of the bunch, were distracted and had to be called twice.

"I want you to know that despite the misbehavior today of some idiot across the street, we will be calm. We will respect the law. We have rights under the laws of this land, and so do the Pintos. The scabs, those interlopers, are citizens of this land and they have rights also. We believe that every individual, no matter who he or she is, has the same rights as any other individual.

We also believe that the fruits of our economic system should be available to all and that everyone has a fundamental right to participate and realize a suitable livelihood. I want to remind everyone that the labor laws of this country decree that no man on this island should be exploited because of a perceived station in life or be forced to labor under conditions that reduce their worth."

Beady could have been reading from a psalter or reciting the Lord's Prayer. His words were authoritative and he connected with his audience. He had practiced some, and was ready to use his little speech as a motivator if needed. The strikers were captivated by his homily and their resolve stiffened.

"Hold the line, the strike is on!" the twelve strikers shouted in unison.

While Beady was motivating his people, the scabs determined that the gallery, which had quickly developed mob tendencies, had become unpredictable and they left as a police Land Rover drove toward the strike location.

"It look like one police jeep coming down the road," Winston said to Patrick as he looked over the crowd into the distance. On the island, jeep was not a brand of auto but a type of auto, and the Land Rover was a jeep.

The gallery saw the blue police vehicle at the same time Winston did. They sounded the alarm before the police jeep parked thirty yards from the strikers. A young man – the same young man who threw the stone at the scab – was loud and unruly, and spewed nastiness with every outburst. He was being warned about his behavior by a retired mason named Eldon, who spent his days visiting the magistrate's court and sitting in on any mêlée he came upon – like the picket.

"This is a free country, me say wha' me like." The young fellow glared at Eldon.

"That might be so, but take it easy; them police don't play," Eldon warned, leaning in and touching him on the elbow. The angry, foul-mouthed youth pulled his arm away.

The police officers left their jeep, closed its doors, put on their hats, and took a leisurely stroll. Three officers, including a supervisor, strolled toward the strikers, while two more officers moved toward the gallery. The smaller of the two officers was first to the gallery, and was first to hear the young fellow oozing expletives. The young man did not know much, nor did he think much, and was unaware that there were laws on the books forbidding the use of "bad words" in public places.

"Sir, what is your name?" the officer demanded, touching a pencil to the tip of his tongue and preparing to write in a small black notebook already in hand. The young man quickly turned his back to the police officer and began to walk away.

"Sir, what is your name? Sir, tell me your name," the officer insisted. He took a step forward, and that was when Foulmouth committed what everyone in Celadon knew was the gravest offence that he could have committed against a police officer: he accidentally knocked off the officer's hat.

The second officer, who had finally arrived at the gallery, was thick and tall and he quickly removed his staff and whacked the young man on the left side of his head. Blood squirted from a wound on the young man's ear, and onto the people nearby. The folks that were tainted with blood hollered, and someone bawled "Murdah!" The crowd tried to scatter, but the three officers who had gone over to the picketers quickly joined the skirmish at the gallery, staffs drawn, and they began to share blows equally among the assembled with no consideration for innocence or guilt.

Word of the bacchanal spread quickly, and the gathering grew to a size larger than the five officers could control. Beady and the picketers left their posts and moved closer to the mêlée, where Beady made a passionate but unproductive attempt to quell the disturbance.

Obstinate acts continued in earnest. Missiles were hurled at the Pinto's building, which was promptly shuttered. The more pigheaded among the crowd were attempting to move the fun to

Uptown, and would have succeeded, but police reinforcements arrived, took control of the situation, and made many arrests. Some were tossed into police jeeps head first. Others were police-walked: grabbed by the belt from behind with an upward jerk, which caused the offenders to tiptoe all the way to the police station. The scene at the end of it was typical for a public disturbance, rampant citizens acting violently and damaging property.

It rained immediately after the arrests, a heavy tropical downpour, sudden, and with large, loud raindrops. It was a fitting end to the day's events, a deluge to cool everyone down and wash the rancor away. The shower did not last long, but the sky remained overcast. The brief storm dumped enough water to back up the gutters and send any lingering spectators to their homes, forcing the outdoor vendors near the market to call it a day.

CHAPTER TWENTY-EIGHT
Encumbered

After things settled down, and after the arrested individuals were processed, a disconsolate Beady headed home. He was glum, tired, and hungry. A meeting was planned at union headquarters the next day to assess the viability of the strike, and to review the disturbance and its cause. Beady had worked with the general secretary to get everyone out of jail, even the folks from the gallery who'd started the disturbance. None of the incarcerated would be kept overnight; everyone had been released, including Walrus and Fidel, who were arrested for obstruction.

The news of the mini-riot traveled quickly around the island, and inevitably, in the ensuing discussions, the police action was looked upon with disfavor; that would have been the case no matter what had transpired between the police and the citizenry or how.

Beady arrived home to a covered dinner plate on the dining table in a troubled house. One of the two women in the house was sniveling, the other was hysterical, and both were distraught. He barely got the essence of their distress before he left the house to hurry up Johnny Hill. He had forgotten that he was hungry, and the covered plate on the table was at the bottom of the list of things on his mind. On his way up the hill, before meeting anyone, he had a few minutes to consider his day and surmised that it couldn't get worse. As bad as it had been, that was a fair assumption.

Halfway up Johnny Hill, Beady's lonely walk and contemplation was interrupted by the sound of a harsh voice.

"Beady, you in the area again?" The question-statement came from Croaky, a middle-aged farmer, whom people said was born hoarse. He was heading in the opposite direction with a pitchfork on his shoulder, but had stopped, expecting to talk.

"Mister Joe, you coming from you grung?" Beady used the man's real name, struggling to sound casual.

"Yes, an' me hear 'bout you little trouble today, but no worry 'bout it; it will work out. You hear?" Mr. Joe said before resuming his journey.

Beady proceeded to make the obligatory visit to his Goddy. He walked up to the house, knocked on the front door, called her name, and then entered.

"Good afternoon, Goddy." Beady's attitude and voice contradicted his emotions at that moment, but he had to be composed for his Goddy. He was still thinking about the mounting troubles in his life when a recollection brought a smile to his lips. The memory was of the halcyon days of Miss Sarah's baker shop and an exchange between Miss Sarah, Lynita's departed mother, and Beady. He replayed the scene in his mind.

"Goodnight, Miss Sarah." Beady's greeting, and his demeanor, was full of respect.

"Goodnight, Tyrone." It was approaching eight o'clock and was quite dark when Beady walked into the grocery section of the baker shop. The presence of electricity and electric lights was occasional then, and it was midweek and past the end of the day for most people.

"I would like to get a sixpence bun, please." Beady placed his order, quietly put his money on the counter, then suddenly shouted. "Miss Sarah, Miss Sarah, wha' he a do in deh?"

The young Beady was shocked, pointing a stiff index finger at the end of a stiff right hand at the glass case where baked goods were displayed. "Wha' he a do in deh?"

"Ah deh he sleep, ah deh he sleep, leave him alone, it's where he sleep," replied Miss Sarah unflappably. She took Beady's money, pulled out her cash drawer to give him change, and barely glanced at her cat taking a nap beside the buns and tarts inside the glass case.

"Tyrone, Tyrone," Goddy Lynita called him into the present and the adult Beady shook off the childhood memory.

"Tyrone, did I ever tell you about you and George?" Lynita said, in a voice that he had not heard for a long time.

"Goddy?" The question puzzled Beady. He hadn't expected his godmother to say much; she never did. She would smile sweetly and nod, thank him when he brought flowers, but seldom did she say much beyond that. She spent most of her active hours in two worlds – one that was and one that could have been.

"Did anyone ever tell you that he is your brother?" Lynita was sitting near a window with a good view from the east side of Johnny Hill, looking out at Celadon below and most of the city beyond. She did not look at Beady when she asked the question, so she did not notice that he was winded. The question was a blow to his celiac plexus and it was some time before he could breathe normally.

"Goddy, you just said that Oxy is my brother. Is that what you wanted to say?"

"Yes, that is what I said, and that is what I wanted to say. You know that he is less than a year younger than you. Well, you mother Cathleen and her best friend Dianne shared more than clothes and shoes. I wanted to tell you this because I think that you need to know."

Lynita's gaze never left the view outside her window.

"But Goddy, how come you never tell me about this before, and why you decided to tell me today?" Beady asked softly.

"Because I was waiting on George's aunt to tell him. After all, George's mother is her sister. His aunt should have been the one to tell him, and then he would tell you. Your mother Cathleen was eight months pregnant with you when Dianne conceived." Beady struggled to process what he was hearing as Lynita continued.

"When Aunty brought my lunch," she said, referencing the fact that Oxy's aunt provided her with meals as reward for a long ago kindness, "she told me about your strike and the commotion that take place today, and it dawned on me that you are an adult now, and that you are man enough to deal with adversity."

Lynita finally looked away from the window, and Beady saw a long-ago look on her face. "It is something that you deserved to know, and for all these years, interacting with all the people who knew this and you not knowing is shameful. If I was the woman that I am supposed to be, then you wouldn't have to experience this ugly circumstance."

She squeezed Beady's left cheek between the index and middle fingers of her right hand, just like she did when he was a child. That gesture always produced a joyful smile and so it did now.

There are three imperatives for a man's survival: to know what is too much for him, what is too little, and what is just enough. When Beady left Goddy's house, he felt like a crumpled man, crushed by the events of the day. The three encumbrances: the strike, his godmother's revelation and the issue he'd inherited when he stopped at his house were weighing him down. However, he chose to continue, and repeated his favorite African proverb: "However long the night may last, there will be a morning."

Back on the road and walking near the center, Beady was startled by a blaring horn, and the car that forced him to the side.

"Oieee, who that?" Beady yelled.

"Hey Beady, you gonna groove with you pal Oxy?" Gutly's wide American car had stopped alongside Beady, who had to step off of the narrow concrete road to make room for it.

"Dig it," Beady responded, automatically slipping into the appropriate idiolect.

Gutly was convinced that a taxi driver needed to be a hipster and use hip American slang. His yanking (mimicking Black American speech) was lost on the tourists he transported. His passengers were mostly mature white folks from the United Kingdom, the United States, and Canada, who hardly understood his counterfeit Yankee blaccent. Nevertheless, his friends indulged him.

"I hear about your trouble with the man." Gutly put a hand out of the car window with the palm up, waiting for a low-five from Beady.

Beady slapped Gutly's outstretched palm before setting him straight about what happened. "No man, just doing my job."

"I hear that someone get a pounding from the fuzz, but I know you cool, and you ain't a momma's boy, and you don't talk no jive," Gutly said cheerfully, before starting his car, tooting his horn, and driving off.

After Gutly left, Beady took a deep breath and continued to walk up the center of the road. As he neared Aunty's gap, he slowed his pace, but he really wanted to slow his swirling thoughts.

CHAPTER TWENTY-NINE
Confrontation

Aunty was preparing for her evening sit down and chat with her neighbors as Beady made his way to her gap. She stood near her back steps, watching a burdened and dejected Oxy walk across the yard, further darkening an overcast afternoon. Oxy extended a barely audible greeting that changed Aunty's demeanor, so she delayed her exit and attempted to lessen the darkness and lighten his load.

"Are you going to eat something before you leave again?" Aunty asked, and smiled before continuing. "If you want something to eat, you came outside at perfect time; I turn some fungee and if you were one minute later you wouldn't want to eat it. You know how the cornmeal that I buy from Mister Butcher get jacket quick," Aunty joked.

With a soft face, she stared at Oxy and waited for a reaction, but Oxy was busy attempting to process the thoughts in his head, and eating was not one. He had plenty to consider following the agonizing talk with Tricia and the possibilities of a life with Rachel and his sons.

"No, Aunty. I don't feel like eating right now." Oxy walked around the stone-heap toward the kitchen as he answered. "I'm sure you make some fever grass tea. Right? I will have some of that."

"Yes, there is some in there, in the kitchen."

Aunty continued to look at Oxy, still with a soft face, waiting on him to share whatever was on his mind. She watched him walk into the kitchen and stayed near the steps, waiting for his return. She intended to remain were she was until she got an answer from her nephew. Oxy returned, holding an enamel cup by the brim. The cup was filled with bush tea and as he took a sip he noticed that his aunt had not moved, and was looking at him, so he decided to unburden himself.

"I'm going to get back with Rachel," he said, his sad eyes meeting hers.

Aunty was aghast, not with horror but with bewilderment. That short statement stirred so many emotions in her: confusion, anger, regret, happiness, sadness. She sat, weakened and quiet on the steps, her right hand touching down first to steady herself. It required five deep breaths before she responded.

"Boy, wha' you talking about, you know wha' you ah say?"

"Yes, Aunty, I know what I am saying. For once I'm taking responsibility and making the right choice, and I know that my decision will bring bitterness and turmoil into my life and the lives of people I care about." Oxy paused, took a sip, sat on the edge of the stone heap across from his aunt, and placed his tea on the ground between his legs. "When I leave here, I'm going to find Beady and talk to him about it. I—"

Oxy's aunt interrupted him before he completed what he wanted to say. "Yes, that is something that you want to do soon." The emotions that had weakened her temporarily and deprived her of speech were replaced by concern.

"He should already know 'bout it, because I talk to Tricia, but I still need to talk to him."

Aunt and nephew sat in the late afternoon quietly discussing his difficulty and her feelings about it. Finally, he stood, returned an empty cup to the kitchen, told her he was leaving, and thanked her for supporting him.

Oxy was turning to go in search of his friend when he heard Beady's voice responding to some inquiry from a busybody on a nearby street. Oxy was set to walk toward Beady's voice, believing that he would need only to give his friend an explanation of his talk with Tricia. He was wrong. Beady's knowledge of the talk amounted to the brief sketch he had gotten from a distraught Tricia, whose temperament precluded extremes, and a hysterical Ruth, whose nature permitted them.

Beady had left the road and was walking along a dirt footpath to Oxy's residence. The path was not level or even, and although it was easy enough to walk along the path when it was dry, whenever it rained the removal of topsoil and the exposure of rocks and stones by rain-wash meant that care was required to traverse it.

"Aunty, excuse me a minute." Oxy began to walk toward the voice when he heard Beady call his name.

"George, before you go, there is something I need to tell you. Them two little boys for my godson Wellesley, they going to come stay with me for a while; that worthless boy drinking again and his woman Gloria acting up."

"Aunty, what you mean Gloria acting up?" Oxy asked.

"You know she head not too good; she was walking about barefoot, talking to she self, she hair no comb, and leaving her sons by themselves. Today the police pick she up and carry she up. Me have to take the children until she get better because Lord knows that she family is no better," Aunty said.

"Okay, Aunty, we can talk about that later. I hope they don't keep Gloria up crazy house too long," Oxy said, and walked away.

"Oxy, hey Oxy, ah wan' see you," Beady called.

"I'm here," Oxy replied. The longtime friends met on the dirt footpath, and stood facing each other.

"Yes, brother, I want to talk to you too. I know you hands full right now, your mind overflowing with the fallout from the strike; I know it's all a big burden," Oxy said, then looked at his friend and sensed trouble.

Beady took a deep breath, held it, and took his time. Oxy knew this meant Beady had something to say but wasn't ready to talk. He waited. It was a discomfiting sight: two men standing facing each other under an overcast evening sky, no words between them. And when Beady finally spoke, he was animated. He did not raise his voice or speak in anger.

"A righteous man who submits to wickedness is like a muddied spring or a polluted well," he quoted scripture, surprising himself by remembering the quote. He had spent many hours at various church services, prayer meetings, and singing meetings as a child, but he'd never been interested in memorizing or reciting scriptures except the golden text, which was the primary takeaway from Sunday school.

"Why are you distraught, my brother? It was just a single bad day brought about by dunces." Oxy attempted to soothe.

"And, Oxy, you believe that is all? You believe that I am in this mindset because of the issues with the strike? There is a lot more going on. Oxy, when did you decide to leave Tricia, and why?" Beady wiped at an itch on his cheek with the back of his hand, and still that was the only movement of either man.

"You know what; forget that I ask you that question," Beady continued earnestly. "Your answer would be irrelevant, useless, 'cause for me what you are doing to Tricia is atrocious. All the love that you professed, all the attention, the drastic changes that a relationship with you brought into her life, why was that?"

Beady put his hand up to signal to Oxy to be quiet as the other man opened his mouth to answer. "I am not finished. She will be affected for life. This is not one of them things that either kill you or fatten you, it only kill and this will impact her attitudes for the rest of her life. I know that she is a strong young woman, but you pursued her relentlessly, and then some more after that, and now you do this."

Beady closed his eyes, took three deep breaths, puffed his chest out and continued. "In case you no notice, me vex with you. For the first time since we met playing in the dirt under Miss Pele tamarind tree, I don't like you." Beady's tone was derisive.

The next sound from Beady's mouth was a snicker, a disrespectful laugh, and then he continued to unload. "I just come from my godmother, Lynita, and she tell me that you are my brother."

Oxy again began to speak, but Beady didn't let him. "Wait, let me finish. She say that we have the same father; that our mothers, good friends that they were, how did she put it, 'your mother Cathleen and her best friend Dianne shared more than clothes and shoes.' Before you say anything, I believe her. She might be a solitary soul but her capabilities are what they always were. The folks that make judgments about her are all nincompoops."

Both men finally moved, Beady first. He walked past Oxy and was two steps ahead and still in a gruff mood before Oxy spoke.

"Beady, you can't just lay all this on me and we don't discuss it," Oxy pleaded. "You just can't walk away from me like that; I said that I want to talk to you. You no le' me say one word; I need to say something."

Oxy stepped up behind Beady, and since both men were the same height, it was an easy reach to touch his brother on the shoulder. Beady turned around, still annoyed, and swung his hand, without looking, in an effort to brush off Oxy's hand. But he misjudged the proximity of Oxy and accidentally hit him in the face. Oxy stepped backward to avoid the full force of the blow and stumbled when his heel came into contact with the stump that his aunt had asked him to remove. Oxy slipped and fell, unable to break his fall, and hit the back of his head on a protruding rock.

"Damn it! Oh shit!" Beady's exclamation was loud, and everyone in the neighborhood heard it. Neighbors began to run to the scene, and everyone was hollering something.

"Somebody bring some Limocal!"

"Somebody call Gutly fo' carry he deh ah hospital!"

"Ah wha' happen?"

*"For Fate with jealous eye does see
Two perfect loves, nor lets them close;
Their union would her ruin be,
And her tyrannic power depose."*
—Andrew Marvell

EPILOGUE

No, Oxy did not die. Gutly had sped to the scene with taxi doors half open, and Oxy was moved to his taxi by the nosy neighbors. He carried Oxy to the hospital, accompanied by Beady and a concerned Aunty, who even in her distress did not overlook hospital clothes (new pajamas and new underwear from the hospital suitcase). The people of Celadon believed that one should have hospital clothes packed and ready (if you went to the hospital, you must at least look decent).

After a month in the hospital, Oxy returned to Celadon weakened, but with improved circumstances. The Jacobses invited Oxy to recuperate at their house, and he agreed. The invitation relieved the impending contention over Aunty's time, because the two young sons of Aunty's godson Wellesley had moved in with her temporarily. Wellesley's woman Gloria never got better.

Beady's strike, although a harrowing experience, was deemed successful after the Pinto's management recognized the union. Beady also won his battle with his ambivalence about his relationship with Sister Ruth after the two little boys for Aunty's godson Wellesley found a permanent home with them, and love returned to their house. However, Beady and his football team had to accept relegation, because the Honorable was not able to persuade the football authorities to come to a different decision.

Tricia never saw Oxy again. She received her papers and left Celadon to join her mother in New York, while her aunt, Sister Allen, dedicated herself to her job, Brother James's ministry, and working hard to project a positive persona.

Palance disappeared on the same day that he had a very loud and public confrontation with a fellow gambler, and he hasn't been seen since. Some say that he went through the window of illegal entry into the U.S., while others speculate about a more inauspicious exodus for the pugnacious man.

The traditions of the Corner haven't changed. Tortoise and Brap migrated to the U.S., but their roles were adequately filled by new players.

The island has suffered from the debauchery of developers – developers who, without foresight, destroyed coastlines, coral reefs, and mangroves. Developers who continue to sacrifice the balance and beauty that nature provided, all the while obliterating the very thing they are attempting to sell. They are smart people who choose to be willfully ignorant of the importance of the natural environment and the relations and interactions among all living things. They complain about over-fishing but continue to pollute the breeding grounds that would allow fish stock to recover. But in spite of all of this, the island remains picturesque in spots.

Next time, I will tell you about my friends and I, and our involvement with AM 610 (The Soul Shack), and the Sunday morning when the police came with their biggest and most disagreeable recruits to raid our little pirate radio station.

Made in the USA
Charleston, SC
16 December 2015